# It's a
# Green
# Thing

"Maya is a fun character! It's not even possible to read *It's a Green Thing* and not relate to her questions, her challenges, and her struggles as a teen and Christian. *And* I found myself jotting down her awesome eco-friendly tips!"

—JENNY B. JONES, award-winning author of *In Between* and the Charmed Life series

### Praise for
### *A Not-So-Simple Life*

"As Maya Stark pours her heart out in her journal, readers are treated to an inside view of a life that is at times exotic and unfamiliar and at other times hauntingly similar to our own. Maya's struggles become our struggles, her pain our pain, and her successes, therefore, even sweeter. *A Not-So-Simple Life* is another triumph for Melody Carlson."

—VIRGINIA SMITH, author of *Sincerely, Mayla* and *Stuck in the Middle*

"Fantastic book! Maya is so easy to like—this is a hard story to put down!"

—ERYNN MANGUM, author of *Miss Match*

"Melody Carlson has proven her skill once again at writing gritty stories about characters in difficult situations. In *A Not-So-Simple Life,* Maya Stark seeks to escape life under the controlling hand of her drug-addicted mother by acting on a plan for independence with admirable determination."

—MICHELLE BUCKMAN, author of *Maggie Come Lately* and *My Beautiful Disaster*

"I just finished Melody's book and loved it! The journal format makes the story, and Maya, so real and believable. Readers will easily be able to identify with the realistic approach to a prevalent situation."

—PATRICIA RUSHFORD, author of the Max & Me Mysteries

Diary of a Teenage Girl

Maya Book No. 2

# It's a Green Thing

a novel

## MELODY CARLSON

MULTNOMAH
BOOKS

It's a Green Thing
Published by Multnomah Books
12265 Oracle Boulevard, Suite 200
Colorado Springs, Colorado 80921

Scripture quotations on pages 55 and 59 are taken from the Contemporary English Version. Copyright © 1991, 1992, 1995 by American Bible Society. Used by permission. The other Scripture quotation on page 55 is taken from God's Word, a copyrighted work of God's Word to the Nations Bible Society. Quotations are used by permission. Copyright 1995 by God's Word to the Nations. All rights reserved.

Italics in Scripture quotations reflect the author's added emphasis.

The characters and events in this book are fictional, and any resemblance to actual persons or events is coincidental.

ISBN: 978-1-60142-118-0

Published in the United States by WaterBrook Multnomah, an imprint of The Doubleday Publishing Group, a division of Random House Inc., New York.

Multnomah and its mountain colophon are registered trademarks of Random House Inc.

Library of Congress Cataloging-in-Publication Data
Carlson, Melody.
  It's a green thing : a novel / Melody Carlson.
      p. cm. — (Diary of a teenage girl. Maya ; book no. 2)
  Summary: Maya writes in her journal about her new-found Christian faith as she struggles with relationship problems and her friend Marissa's partying and dangerous lifestyle. Each chapter ends with a "go green" tip.
  ISBN 978-1-60142-118-0
  [1. Christian life—Fiction. 2. Interpersonal relations—Fiction. 3. Conduct of life—Fiction. 4. Diaries—Fiction.]  I. Title. II. Title: It is a green thing.
  PZ7.C216637Is 2009
  [Fic]—dc22
                                                    2008037958

Printed in the United States of America
2009

10 9 8 7 6 5 4 3 2

## One

## June 9

My cousin Kim gave me a new diary yesterday. She received it for graduation, but she prefers to journal on her computer. "With a security lock, of course," she confessed. Anyway, this nicely bound book (a green product made of recycled materials) seems to be enticing me to write. Especially since I already filled up my old diary, which is safely hidden away in one of my suitcases tucked into the back of the guest room closet. Okay, as both Kim and my uncle keep telling me, "It's *not* the guest room, Maya. It's *your* room." I'm trying to see it that way. But it's not easy. So much about my life is not easy...but I must admit that it's getting better. And I do have hope.

Anyway, since today was rather interesting and the beginning of summer vacation, I will start here. Although to get "here," I need to go back to before the school year ended. I'd been attending Harrison High for several weeks when Mr. Fenton challenged our art class to volunteer for a community project. We'd been invited by the park district to create a mural on a downtown youth center. A lot of kids signed up, and everyone seemed supportive and interested. But today, the first day of the project, Marissa Phillips and I were the only ones to actually show.

"It figures," she said as the two of us stood gazing up at the big, boring wall. The paint was splotchy looking, with random beige smears that resembled a bad case of psoriasis. Probably someone's attempt to hide the graffiti and tagging, although a few offensive words still showed through.

"What do you mean?" I asked.

"That no one else would come."

"Why's that?" I adjusted the twisted strap of my OshKosh overalls. I'd gotten dressed pretty quickly this morning, barely managing to catch the downtown bus.

"Because people are basically selfish."

I turned and looked at her. With hands planted on her hips, Marissa stared at the ugly wall and frowned. For some reason, when I first began attending Harrison High, I felt drawn to this girl. Like we shared some commonality. And I suppose we do have some physical similarities. We're both tall and have long hair, although hers is straight and mine is curly. And because she dyes it black, her hair's a lot darker than mine. I think that's why her complexion looks so pale. Whereas mine (thanks to my dad) is the color of café au lait.

But our looks aside, we are similar in other ways too. Or maybe we both just have an attitude. She's not afraid to speak her mind and has opinions that not everyone shares. She's two years older than I am. In fact, she just graduated with my cousin Kim.

Not that she seems older exactly. Or maybe I just feel older than sixteen. Sometimes I feel like I'm in my thirties. But a hard life can do that to a person.

"So if that's true," I asked Marissa, "if people are basically selfish, why are you here?"

She laughed. "I thought you knew."

"Knew?"

"I'm doing community service."

"For what?"

"Oh...something that happened a couple of months ago. I guess you hadn't moved here yet."

"What did you do?"

"I got caught with alcohol in my car."

"Driving under the influence?" I knew Marissa was kind of a wild child, but I thought she had more sense than that.

"No." She shook her head firmly. "I wasn't under the influence. I was underage."

"Well, obviously."

"It didn't really help much that my dad's a cop." She made a face as she reached into her bag and retrieved a pack of cigarettes. She shook one out, quickly lit it, then blew out an exasperated puff.

"Your dad's a cop?" Now this caught me off guard. Of all people who might have law enforcement officials in their family, Marissa just doesn't seem to fit the profile. I can only imagine how frustrated her father must feel.

"Oh yeah..." She peered back at the wall. "In fact it was his recommendation that I spend my summer vacation performing community service. If dear old Dad hadn't been in court that day, I probably would've gotten off a lot easier."

"You're doing community service for the whole summer?"

"Yep." She blew another puff of smoke over her shoulder.

"And you're okay with that?"

"It was either that or give up my car and move out of the house. And I wasn't financially ready for that...not just yet." She took in a slow drag, then looked curiously at me. "So what's your excuse?"

"Excuse?"

"For being here."

"You mean because I must be basically selfish too?"

She shrugged.

"I just wanted to do it," I admitted. "I mean, when Mr. Fenton described the project, it sounded kind of fun to help someone else, and he made it seem like it would only take a week."

Marissa laughed sarcastically. "Yeah, right. Think again."

I frowned back up at the wall. "With just the two of us, this mural could end up being your entire summer of community service."

"I wouldn't mind so much, except that it's going to be scorching out here before long, and this wall is in the sun most of the day." She reached in her bag again, and this time pulled out her cell phone.

"Who are you calling?"

"Friends... Hey, Spencer," she said warmly. "What's up, dude?" Then she winked at me. "Well, Maya and I are downtown right now. We volunteered to do this mural project, and we sure could use some big, strong guys to help out." She smiled knowingly. "Oh yeah, for sure. Maybe you could get Jake to come and help too... No, it's no big hurry. I mean, we need to kind of figure out where we're going with this mural and get the paint and stuff. Maybe not today. But how about tomorrow? First thing in the morning?" She got a catty smile now. "Oh yeah, totally." Then she hung up.

"Help on the way?"

"Sounds like it." She slipped her phone back into her bag. "Spencer is such a pushover when it comes to good-looking women."

"I hope he didn't get the wrong impression."

"We're talking about Spencer, right?" She laughed. "Of course he has the wrong impression. It's just the way that boy's brain is wired."

And I was fully aware of this. Spencer had begun hitting on me as soon as I started going to HHS a couple of months ago. I'd been flattered at first, but as I got to know him better, I realized that I needed to draw some boundaries. Even so, I wasn't going to admit that Spencer wouldn't have been my first choice for help. "So...do you think I should call anyone else?" I offered.

"Sure. Do you know anyone else?"

I kind of shrugged. The truth is, I still don't know that many people in this town. Kim and her best friend, Natalie, already have summer jobs. But I was thinking about the kids in Kim's church youth group—particularly Dominic. Any excuse to spend time with Dominic seemed like a good excuse to me. But I didn't know his number, so I called Caitlin. She and her husband, Josh, are the youth leaders, and she's been sort of mentoring me since I committed my life to God a couple of weeks ago. She answered, and I quickly explained the mural project and our lack of volunteers.

"It was supposed to take only a week," I said finally. "But with just Marissa and me and this great big wall, well, it's a little overwhelming. She's already called a guy to help, but—"

"What a cool project," Caitlin said. "That building is a real eyesore. It's great that someone wants to make it nice, and I'm sure that'll be a blessing to the kids who use the center. Why don't I call around and see who might be willing to help out?"

"That'd be awesome, Caitlin."

"When do you want your helpers to show up?"

"We have to figure some things out first. We probably won't need anyone until tomorrow morning."

"I'll see what I can do."

"Thanks." I hung up and smiled hopefully.

But Marissa was frowning at me now. "Why are you calling in the church people?"

"Why not?"

"You want me to make you a list of reasons?"

"Are you willing to turn away free help?"

She dropped her cigarette butt to the pavement and ground it out with her heel as she shrugged. "I guess not. So what's the deal, Maya? Are you *one of them?*"

"One of what?"

"Are you a Christian too?"

I took in a deep breath, then slowly nodded. "Actually, I am."

She shook her head in a dismal way. Like this was really unfortunate.

"I'll admit it's still kind of new for me," I said.

"Why?" Her dark eyes narrowed as she studied me closely. I started to feel like a bug beneath a magnifying glass.

"Why?" I repeated, confused. "You mean why is it new for me?"

"No. *Why did you do it?*" The way she said this made a woman walking through the parking lot glance nervously at me, like she assumed I'd committed some horrendous crime.

"Become a Christian?"

"Yeah." Marissa made a sour face. "I mean, I can understand girls like Kim and Natalie... They're such goody two-shoes. But you, Maya? I thought you were different."

"I *am* different."

"Then *why?*"

"Because I was unhappy and lonely and hopeless and depressed and just really, really lost."

"And now you're found?" I could hear the teasing note in her voice.

"Actually, I do feel kind of found."

She rolled her eyes.

"Look, Marissa, if anyone had told me just a few months ago that I was going to make a life-changing commitment like this... well, I would've reacted just like you. I would've said they were crazy. Seriously, I never would've believed it myself."

Her countenance softened ever so slightly, and she didn't question this statement.

"And like I said, it's still new to me. Basically, all I can say is that I was totally mixed-up and messed up and just plain lost...and now I have this real sense of peace. Honestly, it's something I never had before."

"Peace?"

I nodded eagerly. "Yes. It's hard to describe it, but it's like my life is in good hands now, like I feel hopeful."

"You sound like Chloe Miller now."

I smiled. "I'll take that as a compliment." The fact is, of all the Christians I know, which aren't that many, I can relate to Chloe best. I mean, Kim is cool and takes her faith seriously. And Caitlin is sweet and sincere and helpful. And Nat... Well, don't get me going there. But right from the start, I seemed to get Chloe. And she seemed to get me. Maybe it has to do with the whole music thing—a kind of artistic, outside-the-box sort of thing.

"So what do you think we should paint on this wall?" Marissa seemed eager to change the subject, and I felt relieved.

"I'm thinking we should get some sketches going." I unzipped my pack and retrieved a sketch pad. "We're not supposed to do anything out here without Mrs. Albert's approval."

"Who's that?"

"The superintendent. But if we can get her okay, we could probably start putting the drawing on the wall before our other volunteers show up. That way we can put them to work."

"Yes sir." She gave me a cheesy grin. "You the boss."

Before long we were sitting there on the curb, discussing ideas and playing with images. Unfortunately, Marissa's ideas leaned toward the dark side, and when I challenged a particularly frightening image, she seemed slightly offended.

"So what do you want to paint?" she shot back. "Sunshine, flowers, and sweet turtledoves?"

"No, not exactly. But something more cheerful than a dragon burning a gnarled tree stump."

"I was just trying to come up with something that graffiti artists would respect," she said defensively. "Something they wouldn't make fun of and want to deface."

"That's a good point. We don't want it to be too childish."

"But I suppose a dragon might be scary to some of the little kids who come here."

"What exactly is the purpose of this building?" I ventured.

She shrugged. "It's a youth center. Duh."

"So it's a place for kids to come...for what purpose?"

"To hang. To play. For kids who need something like that."

I kind of frowned at her. "Why?"

"You know, it's for kids who might be kind of underprivileged, or maybe they're unsupervised. The center has a day-care program and all kinds of classes and activities for after-school programs. Stuff like that." Now she laughed. "Oh yeah, I guess you wouldn't have had anything like that back in Beverly Hills, little Miss Rich Girl."

Sometimes I wish I hadn't told Marissa so much about myself. But at the time, when I needed a friend a couple of months ago, it seemed right. And I thought I could trust her. Not that I can't.

"I'm not a rich girl."

"Says you."

I just rolled my eyes. The truth was, I would've appreciated a center like this when I was a kid. Not that I plan to admit that to Marissa. But despite her misconceptions, my childhood wasn't exactly ideal or nurturing, and I certainly never felt rich. Of course, Beverly Hills isn't the sort of town where people are terribly concerned over the welfare of the younger generation. Like Marissa, people just assume that if you live there, your parents have lots of money, and you'll be just fine.

"So it sounds like it's a place that's meant to encourage kids, to help them grow into better people, to give them hope," I finally said.

Marissa laughed loudly. "Hey, maybe you should go into politics or public relations or advertising or something."

"Come on. The sooner we figure this out, the sooner we can

get some serious sketches going. And the sooner we can get started, the sooner we can get done, and we won't be out here baking in the sun all summer."

"You seem to have it all figured out, boss. Go for it." Marissa pulled out another cigarette.

Now I was tempted to point out the risks of emphysema and lung cancer, as well as how smoke makes your hair stink and yellows your fingernails, but I figured she was probably already aware of these facts.

"Fine. I think we should create something that feels hopeful." I squinted up at the blotchy-looking wall again. "Something colorful and cheerful and happy."

"Maybe we could paint a *pwetty wainbow?*"

Just before I made a smart retort, I stopped myself. "Hey, maybe you're right." I grabbed my sketch pad and began to draw. "But we'll design it in a more modern style. Sort of cubist." She looked over my shoulder as I drew a series of sharply angled shapes, working them together to make an arch.

"Interesting...," she finally admitted.

"Really?"

"Yeah. I can kind of see it. And it would actually be fairly easy to put a team to work on it since it's mostly shapes."

"Exactly. We'll draw them out, and they can paint them in."

"We'll need a lot of different colors."

"So you can see the rainbow?" I asked. "I mean, since there's no color in my sketch?"

"Yeah. I get where you're going." She snuffed out her cigarette, then reached in her bag for a tin of colored pencils. "Here, add some color."

By midmorning we had a final colored sketch as well as Mrs. Albert's approval. "Very nice, girls," she told us as we were ushered out of her office. "And anything will be an improvement over what's out there now."

"Well, that was flattering," Marissa said as we headed down to the storage room to meet the janitor and check out the ladders and painting supplies.

"At least her expectations aren't too high."

Marissa laughed. "Yeah, I'm pretty good at meeting people's *low* expectations."

I wanted to ask her why that was, but we needed to get busy if we were going to put more volunteers to work tomorrow. And to my relief, Marissa actually knew how to work hard. By the end of the day, Marissa had gotten the paints, and I had managed to get a fair amount of the sketch onto the lower part of the wall.

"Nice work, boss," Marissa said after we'd put the supplies away and stood looking at the beginning of our mural.

"Same back at you." And I have to admit that I was kind of excited to see how this whole thing would turn out. And hopefully more people will show up to help tomorrow.

# Maya's Green Tip for the Day

Don't pour harmful wastes down public waterways. Storm drains on public streets are for rainwater to run off so the streets don't flood. They're not a convenient way for people to get rid of chemicals or solvents or even the bucket of soapy water after you wash your car. Unless you use bio-friendly car-wash detergent, which I highly recommend. You need to respect that the water that runs off our streets eventually winds up in streams and waterways and can harm innocent fish or other marine wildlife. So don't use your street drain as a dumping spot.

# Two

## June 10

A s it turned out, we had a crew of seven workers this morning. Okay, not first thing. But by the time Marissa and I had gotten the ladders and scaffolding in place, the other five had arrived, and we put them to work applying paint. I was sketching fast, trying to get the outline of the mural onto the wall, with Marissa following me, chalking in numbers that we had prematched with colors for our painters to fill in.

"It's a kind of paint-by-number thing," I explained, trying not to stare at the odd assortment of volunteers. First there was Spencer, a hard-case dude with a reputation for all kinds of stuff, and his buddy Jake, who still has some rough edges himself, although he's a Christian. And then we had three clean-cut, preppy-looking church kids that Caitlin had managed to talk into helping us. To my dismay, Dominic was not among them. However, one of these kids turned out to be a quiet but hard-working guy named Matt Stephens. How he got mixed up with the other two, a couple of airheaded girls, was a mystery.

Okay, I know it's wrong to call Brooke Marshall and Amanda Groves airheads, but even though they're part of the youth group, they're not exactly the kind of girls I've been dying to get to know better. Unfortunately, they remind me of Kim's buddy Natalie. Meaning they talk too much, have opinions that I don't necessarily agree with, and seem to think they are better than everyone else. Okay, that's my honest take on it. And this is my diary, so I can say what I like!

Anyway, by noon it seemed that our ground crew of five painters was making progress. The color was going up, and despite Brooke and Amanda questioning stupid things like whether number seven was fuchsia or magenta, we were doing okay. Matt was a pretty fast painter, and Jake seemed willing to work, but Spencer acted like this was supposed to be a big party, and he spent most of his time harassing either Marissa or me (or perhaps he thought he was flirting). He kept a safe distance from the "church girls," as he called them. And naturally, they were quick to point out anything that Spencer was doing wrong. Of course, he made this easy for them. And I suppose I don't really blame him. Brooke and Amanda seemed to invite it.

But tonight as I write this, I'm a little concerned. I'm wondering, as a Christian, whether it's wrong to have bad feelings toward other Christians. There's no denying that Brooke and Amanda are Christians. They've made that pretty clear. But at the same time, I don't really want to be associated with them. And then I feel guilty. I guess I'll have to ask Caitlin for some clarification on this. Because the truth is, Brooke and Amanda make me want to run in the opposite direction or maybe just scream some loud obscenity like Spencer does.

"Don't use the Lord's name in vain," Brooke corrected him—over and over today. And it seemed that the more she said this, the worse he got.

"Hey, Spencer," I called. "Maybe you should come up here and work." I thought some space between him and the church girls might help.

His eyes lit up. "Yeah, babe, I'd like that."

"Great." I climbed down the ladder. "Go for it."

"I thought we were both going to be working up there."

"Like you really wanted to work with her," scolded Amanda. "We know what you are up to."

And so it went. Oh, it's not just that these girls seemed afraid to get their hands dirty or break a nail—although that was the case at first. But they had this superior attitude. I'm not sure if it's because they're Christians or because they just honestly believe they're better than the rest of us, but it was like they were doing us this huge favor by lowering themselves to help out today. Such saintly servants of the Lord. Really, someone should've just handed them their crowns and sent them packing. Quite honestly, I hope they don't come back tomorrow. And unfortunately, I have no doubt that Marissa feels the same.

Anyway, it was a relief to call it a day. Although even that started another disagreement. "Don't pour that down there!" I yelled at Brooke. She was about to pour a bucket of sludgy paint water down the street grate.

"What?" She looked up in surprise.

"There's paint in there."

"So?"

"So that grate is for rainwater runoff."

"So?" Now she gave me a defiant stare.

"So the paint in there will harm fish and plant life."

Brooke just laughed, and before I could stop her, she poured it down.

"Brooke! What are you doing?"

"The fish won't mind a little paint in—"

"That is so wrong!" I went over and looked down on her. She's this petite little blond thing (a gymnast, she's told us several times). "Don't ever do that again. Do you understand?"

"Don't get so worked up, Maya." But she took a couple of steps back like she thought I was going to hit her. Okay, maybe I felt like hitting her, but I would never do something like that.

"And quit being so mean to Brooke." This came from Amanda, who was standing by her friend now.

"I'm not being mean," I said as calmly as I could. "I just think we should show some respect for the environment."

Brooke laughed. "What are you? Some kind of environmental freak? A green bean?"

"A tree-hugger?" added Amanda.

Well, all I could do was just walk away. Still, I plan to stand my ground on not contaminating the environment. To my surprise, Marissa, Spencer, and Jake all backed me on this—although it's possible that it was simply their way of standing against Brooke and Amanda. I think Matt was afraid to say anything. Mostly I'm hoping that Brooke and Amanda won't show tomorrow.

After Marissa dropped me at Kim and my uncle's house (I still have a hard time calling it home, although I want to), I was still feeling grumpy. And when I saw Kim putting something in the garbage can, well, I kind of lost it.

"What are you doing?"

"Huh?" Her dark eyes grew large. "Taking out the trash."

"But is that really trash?" I pulled an empty tomato soup can off the top of the bag in her hands. "This can be recycled."

She shrugged. "Yes, I know that."

"And this." I grabbed an empty peanut butter jar.

"Yes…" She frowned.

"And these newspapers?" I pulled a section of the news out, sending garbage tumbling onto the garage floor. "I can use these to compost with." I've already been scavenging items for the compost station out in the garden. Although my uncle has been forgetting and throwing his used coffee grounds down the sink. But this morning I told him that coffee grounds can mess up his plumbing, and he seemed to listen.

Kim made a face at me. "Looks like I've been arrested by the EP."

"EP?"

"Environmental Police." She set down the garbage bag. "Do you plan to lock me up, or can I get off with just a fine?"

I forced a smile. "Sorry, I guess I came on a little strong." Then I told her about Brooke. "I guess I'm hypersensitive today." I looked down at the spilled trash. "And this is your house. I really don't have any—"

"Look, Maya…" Kim paused. "You're absolutely right to care about the environment. And I totally agree with you."

"You do?"

"Yes. Except that recycling takes time. And I work all day. And then there are household chores and dinner and—"

"And I should help out more," I said, feeling guilty.

"No, you've been helping a lot."

"How about I take over the trash detail? I could separate recyclables and make a system that's easy for everyone to use."

She nodded. "That would be awesome, Maya. I'm sure Dad would appreciate it too."

So that's just what I did. And it probably sounds crazy to some people, but getting everything all organized actually felt really good to me. Okay, maybe it was one small step for Maya Stark, but it was one giant leap for the Peterson household—and not bad for the environment either. To start with, I retrieved several old five-gallon buckets from my aunt's garden shed. I cleaned them up and clearly labeled them. One for glass. One for metal. One for soda cans that can be returned to the store for a refund. One for newspapers. Then I called the garbage service to find out if and when they pick up these things. As it turned out, they don't. And I thought that was wrong. So I approached my uncle.

"I can't believe your town doesn't encourage recycling," I said as I showed him my new system. "Lots of sanitation businesses offer special boxes for their customers to use to separate their recyclables."

To my surprise he wholeheartedly agreed with me. And he appreciated that I'd set them up to recycle. "Maybe there's a way we can encourage this through the newspaper," he said. "Because you're right. We need to catch up with the times here."

And so, despite the irritation of people like Brooke Marshall, I am feeling hopeful. There are people who are concerned about the planet. And really, shouldn't Christians be extra concerned? I mean, they know the God who created the planet. Doesn't that make them want to take special care of it?

# Maya's Green Tip for the Day

It's easy to create your own home recycling center. First, decide where to put it and determine how much room you have. Then find some containers large enough to hold your recyclables. I recommend containers that are washable like garbage cans or wastebaskets, but you can use a cardboard box or grocery sack lined with a plastic trash bag. Clearly mark the containers: Glass, Metal, Newspapers, Redeemable Containers, Reusable Bags. The keys to making this work are a handy location, clearly marked containers, and diligence.

# Three

## June 11

Today, the third day of the mural project, my patience wore extremely thin. Not only were Brooke and Amanda making me miserable, but they also managed to drive off Spencer and Jake. Now I'm not terribly surprised that Spencer left, since he didn't really seem to get the work ethic, plus he wasn't making any headway with Marissa or me. But I was disappointed that these two girls were able to offend Jake. Because he is actually a Christian too. I'm pretty sure he got fed up with their "preaching" and as a result never returned after our lunch break. Who could blame him after they actually questioned his faith?

"Why do you have that evil-looking tattoo?" Brooke asked when Jake rolled up his sleeve and she caught sight of the dragon image on his arm.

"What makes it evil?" Marissa paused from mixing a can of paint and glared at Brooke. "I happen to think dragons are pretty cool."

"Yuck," Amanda said. "Dragons are a sign of the devil."

"Says who?" Jake said.

I was perched on a piece of scaffolding, trying to focus on my sketching. Not that it was easy to ignore them.

"Everyone knows that dragons are satanic," Brooke said. "The Bible says so."

"Where in the Bible does it say that?" Jake said.

"I don't know where exactly," spouted Brooke. "I just know it's there."

"Besides," Amanda said, "I can't imagine why anyone would want a dragon permanently imprinted on his body."

"Or any image, for that matter," Brooke added. "Tattoos are evil."

"So dragons are evil, and tattoos are evil," Jake said. "Does that mean I'm evil too?"

"It means you're inviting evil in," Amanda declared.

"How can you possibly know that?" I questioned from up high. I glanced at Marissa now. She just rolled her eyes and dabbed on a spot of magenta. But suddenly I wanted to apologize to her for questioning her dragon sketch on Monday. In fact, I almost wished we had decided to use it after all. Brooke and Amanda certainly wouldn't have offered to help with something that "evil."

"Because it's obvious," Brooke said. "Just look at dragons, and you'll know they're evil."

"Who made you the expert on dragons?" I shot down at them. "And what about Puff the magic dragon? Was he evil?" Then I started loudly singing the old folk song, and Marissa and Jake joined in with me, and I hoped that would be the end of it. But as soon as we stopped singing for lack of lyrics, Brooke started in again.

"You see?" she said in that superior tone. "Puff was magic, and everyone knows that magic is evil."

"Where do you come up with this stuff?" I demanded, ready to engage.

"It's a well-known fact that dragons and magic and witches and all those things are evil," declared Amanda.

Fortunately, it was around noon by then, and Matt, who until then hadn't said a word, suggested we take a lunch break. I was actually hoping that Brooke and Amanda would be offended enough by our dragon position to call it a day and not come back. But as I mentioned, it was Jake and Spencer who didn't return. And for Jake's sake, and ours, I felt sorry.

"If we weren't so desperate to get this project done, I'd tell those two girls to take a hike," Marissa whispered as we both stood on the scaffolding scrutinizing the mural's progress this afternoon. I was drawing, and she was following behind me, keying in the paint colors. Our new time-saving strategy was to sketch the outlines, then put dots of color so the "painters" knew what color to paint the various shapes. So far, other than religious differences, it all seemed to be turning out just fine.

"I know," I muttered. "And if it makes you feel any better, I'm sorry I called in the church people."

"See, you should've listened to me."

"But Matt is nice."

"I think he's an anomaly."

"And me?"

She nodded. "Yes. Both of you."

"Another thing," I said quietly. "I'm sorry about something else."

"What?"

"That I rejected your dragon suggestion."

She snickered. "Can you imagine Brooke and Amanda painting that evil image?"

"My point exactly." I glanced down to where the preacher girls were working on a section of varying shades of purple.

Marissa shrugged. "Well, whether we like them or not, they've actually turned out to be fairly good painters."

"I suppose."

"So if we can just avoid talking about dragons and witches, maybe we'll survive this and be done with it in a few more days."

"Hello up there," called a guy's voice.

I looked down to see Dominic and another guy I didn't recognize waving at us.

"Dominic!" Brooke ran over and threw herself at him in a big hug. "I'm so glad you came."

Okay, I have to wonder why some girls think it's acceptable to literally throw themselves at a guy that way. Is it because they're cute and petite and assume that every guy can't wait to get his arms around them? I'm just not comfortable acting like that. Plus there's always the chance for rejection.

But Amanda was right there too, hugging Dominic with equal enthusiasm and warmly greeting his friend, who was actually rather good-looking too. Not as handsome as Dominic, who could pass for a young Johnny Depp with blue eyes, although I think Dominic's taller.

"Are you guys here to help us?"

"You bet," Dominic said. "Hey, Maya, how's it going?"

"Pretty good. You're really here to paint?"

"Of course," Brooke said in that I-know-it-all voice. "I'm the one who called and invited him in the first place."

"And this is my new friend, Eddie Valdez." Dominic introduced Eddie to everyone, including Marissa, which surprised me. I didn't know Dominic actually knew her by name. "Eddie's family just moved next door to us. And I coerced him to come and help with this project."

"Cool," Brooke said. "We're in need of some *good* workers."

I wanted to point out this was only because she and Amanda had driven the others away, but I managed to bite my tongue. Still, as the afternoon wore on, it wasn't easy to keep my thoughts to myself. From the way Brooke spoke to Dominic and Eddie, you'd have assumed that she was in charge of the entire project. It's like she wanted to take the credit for everything. And that irked me.

"The children who use this building are really going to like this mural," she said when Dominic complimented the design.

"It's colorful and fun, and of course you probably know that the rainbow is a Christian symbol."

"What's that you're saying about the rainbow?" Marissa said from up high on the scaffolding.

"That it's a religious symbol," Brooke said. "Surely you know that."

"I know that it's a symbol used by the homosexual community," Marissa said in a slightly smug voice. "Also there's the human rights Rainbow Coalition."

"Well, that's only because they stole it from the church."

"They *stole* it?" said Marissa. "Wow, how does someone go about stealing a rainbow? And how does someone else claim ownership of a rainbow in the first place?"

"You should try reading the Bible," said Amanda. "It explains a lot of things."

"Along with the dragons, I suppose," said Marissa.

"You guys don't want to pay too much attention to Marissa." Brooke directed this to Dominic and Eddie. "She's not a Christian, you know. And she thinks dragons and magic and all that are perfectly fine."

"Yes," said Marissa. "You little girls better watch out. I'm probably a witch too. I might cast a spell on you." She waved her paintbrush like a wand as if to prove her point.

Okay, I couldn't help but laugh at that. Although Brooke and Amanda didn't think it was very funny, and I'm not sure what Dominic and Eddie thought. But I decided the best thing to do was to return my focus to my drawing. What was the point in arguing with people like Brooke and Amanda? Who knows how their minds work? Or if they even do.

But I do know this. The sooner that mural gets done, the happier I'll be. Still, I can't help but wonder about "Christians" who act like that. I mean, aren't Christians supposed to love everyone? That's what I recall the members in my grandmother's church saying, back when I was little. At least I think that's how it went. Perhaps I've gotten things mixed up over the years. Anyway, it seems I have lots of questions... I just hope I can find some answers.

## June 12

As it turned out, Matt Stephens only lasted two days on the mural. Brooke said this was because he got a real job, but I have to wonder if he wasn't just getting sick of Brooke and Amanda. Or maybe he got sick of all of us since there's been a lot of arguing going on. Anyway, he was a hard worker, and he'll be missed. Still, I'm glad that Dominic and Eddie seem to be sticking with it.

Marissa has been giving me rides downtown this week. And while her car is a bit of a junkyard (she uses the backseat as a trash receptacle), it does beat riding the bus. Plus it's more fuel efficient for her to share a ride than to drive alone. Of course, she only laughed when I told her this.

"You really are a green girl, aren't you?"

"I take conservation and the earth seriously," I said. "Don't you?"

"I guess I don't really think about it much."

"Maybe you should."

She nodded, like she was considering this. "But it's weird because I don't usually think of Christians as very environmentally conscious."

"Why not?"

"Well, take people like Brooke and Amanda..."

I sighed. "Don't remind me."

"They don't seem to care about the environment. In fact, they don't seem to care about much of anything besides being right and telling everyone else how to live and what to think. Kind of like the religious mind police."

"But you don't think all Christians are like that, do you? I mean like the religious mind police?"

"Well, I don't think you are. Neither is Chloe. Or Allie either. I used to think Laura had a superiority complex, but after being in the band, she changed."

"I don't know Allie and Laura that well," I admitted as I tried to remember my first impressions of Chloe's band members. I wasn't a Christian when I first met them, but Allie had struck me as laid-back and friendly, and Laura seemed quiet and thoughtful. Neither had come across as judgmental. "But they seem okay to me." Mostly I wanted to remind Marissa that not all Christians are like Brooke and Amanda.

"And your cousin, Kim, is okay. But Natalie...well, she's a piece of work."

"Maybe Christians are just like everyone else," I mused. "Some are cool, and some are—"

"Jerks?"

"I was going to say not so cool. Maybe we're all kind of like the mural."

"How's that?" asked Marissa.

"Works in progress. But maybe some of us are a little further along than others."

"I guess."

Still, even as I said this, I wasn't so sure. In fact, the longer I'm a Christian, which admittedly hasn't been long at all, the more unsure I feel about a lot of things. But I can't deny that I still have that peace. I've been taking time to pray (Caitlin said that's my life-line), and I've been reading the Bible as well as a book that's supposed to help explain some things. I'll meet with Caitlin again on Saturday morning. I might bring a list of questions with me.

"How's your dad doing?" Marissa asked straight out of the blue. She and I were adjusting the ladders and the board that serves as a scaffold between them.

"Huh?" I peered curiously at her, almost wishing I'd never confided in her in the first place. Thankfully, I'd never mentioned that my mom was in prison, but I did let a few other things slip, including the short touring stint I'd done with Dad last winter. Maybe I just needed someone to talk to, someone I thought I could trust. But when she found out about my dad's music career and how I liked to keep it low-key, she'd been cool with it.

"He's okay," I murmured, glancing down to see if anyone was listening to us. But the other four seemed preoccupied with painting.

"Well, I looked up his Web site last night."

"Really?"

"Yeah. I was trying to make some points with *my* dad."

"How's that?"

"Well, you know, this whole summer is going to be such a drag. So anyway, my dad's a Nick Stark fan, and I told him he was your dad and—"

"Your dad is Nick Stark?" Eddie said suddenly.

I tossed Marissa a warning look, but she just shrugged. "What's the big deal, Maya?"

"Who's Nick Stark?" Brooke said.

"He's a rock star," Eddie told her. Then he looked at me. "Seriously, is Nick Stark really your dad?"

"He's more like a *pop* star," I said. "And kind of a has-been at that." It's not that I'm not proud of Dad. I guess I sort of am. But having grown up in Beverly Hills, I learned early on not to make a big deal of my dad's music career. There was always someone with a parent far more famous and a lot richer than mine. I learned to keep a low profile.

"Rock star, pop star, whatever," Eddie said eagerly. "Is he really your dad, Maya?"

I nodded, then returned my attention to adjusting the scaffold.

"Wow, that is so cool," Eddie said. "My parents are huge fans."

"So is my dad," Marissa said. "And now my dad wants to meet you, Maya."

"Oh..." I nodded as I climbed down the ladder.

"So how famous is he?" asked Brooke.

"How do you measure famous?" I opened a can of number eleven, electric blue paint.

"You know," Brooke persisted. "Is he like a-household-word famous?"

"Sounds like he's not one in your house."

Brooke laughed. "That's because my parents only listen to Christian music."

"That's too bad," said Marissa.

"I've heard of Nick Stark," Dominic said. "But I don't think I've heard his music."

"It's kind of the typical seventies-eighties stuff," I told them.

"So where does he live?" asked Brooke. "And why aren't you with him?"

"Right now I'm staying with my uncle and cousin for a while. And my dad lives, well, on the road."

"On the road?" Brooke frowned. "Is he homeless?"

Marissa threw back her head and laughed loudly. "Yeah, right. What you don't know could fill a library, Brooke."

"You don't have to be mean."

"He's touring," I told her. "Doing concerts. At the moment he's in Europe—Sweden, I think."

"And Maya could be with him," added Marissa.

"Wow," Dominic said. "Why aren't you?"

I considered this. So many possible answers.

"Yeah, why aren't you?" pestered Brooke.

"Because I'm not. I toured with him for a while, and it got old pretty quick. I just want a normal life. And to be honest, I'd appreciate it if you guys didn't talk about my dad. Okay?"

Of course Brooke and Amanda kept pounding me with questions, all of which seemed money related. It was obvious that material wealth was important to them, but I was evasive. Finally Dominic managed to get them to stop.

"Give Maya a break," he said. "She's here to paint—not to give you guys her family history!"

"Yeah," Eddie agreed. "Just because her dad's famous doesn't mean she's public property. You two are acting just like the paparazzi."

I had to chuckle at that. But at least it shut them up.

# Maya's Green Tip for the Day

Today I'm thinking about paint. Since we're painting out-
doors, we're not too worried about paint fumes. But if
you redecorate your bedroom, painting the walls or
pieces of furniture, you should be aware that some paint
fumes can be toxic. And indoor air pollution caused by
using the wrong products can be many times worse
than outdoor air pollution. So if you're buying interior
paint, choose either low VOC paints or non-VOC paints.
(VOC stands for volatile organic compounds, and they
are not good for you.) Better yet, why not try natural
paints (made from things like milk protein, clay, or lime)?
These products might cost a little more, but, hey, your
lungs and your health are worth it!

## Four

**June 13**

Do you know what today is?" Marissa asked everyone as we were getting ready to start painting again this morning.

"Friday?" I ventured. I'd been hoping we could finish the mural today.

*"Friday the thirteenth,"* she said in a spooky voice, like maybe she thought she could unnerve Brooke and Amanda or frighten them away, which would actually be unfortunate since without their help there's no way we'd finish today.

"So?" Brooke looked blankly at Marissa. "Christians aren't superstitious."

"Really?" Marissa looked skeptical. "Then why do you wear that cross around your neck? That's not superstition?"

"No. The cross is a symbol of faith." Brooke fingered her golden cross.

"That's right," Amanda said. "You're the one who's superstitious, Marissa."

"Well, be careful walking under these ladders," warned Marissa. "Could be bad luck."

"There's no such thing as bad luck," Amanda pointed out.

"What about bad karma?" Marissa said.

"None of that applies to a Christian," Brooke said in a slightly superior tone. "Bad luck or karma or any of those superstitious things."

"Meaning bad things don't happen to Christians?" Okay, I hadn't meant to get involved, but I just couldn't help myself.

Dominic laughed. "Hey, ladies. Why don't you all give the religious war a break today?"

"We're not at war," Brooke said defensively. "We're just trying to enlighten some people."

"You're right, Dominic," I said quickly. "Let's declare the rainbow mural as a peace zone for the entire day."

"I'm in." Marissa nodded as she opened a can of fuchsia paint.

"You got my vote," added Eddie.

"And if we give this wall everything we've got," I said, "we might even finish today." I looked up at the mural and tried to imagine it finished. At that moment it looked like a giant jigsaw puzzle with lots and lots of missing pieces. But if we all did our parts, there was a chance we'd finish. So just as I'd done on the previous mornings, I began assigning painting positions. It kept us from stepping on each other or getting in the way.

"Why do Amanda and I always get stuck on the ground level?" demanded Brooke.

"Stuck on the ground?"

"Yeah. You and Marissa always hog the ladders and the scaffolding," Amanda said.

"We've been up there too," Dominic said.

"Maybe it's our turn to work on top," Brooke said.

"Fine," I told her. "I don't mind working down here."

"Me either." Marissa shrugged. "I think it's cooler down here anyway."

"Just be careful," I warned them. "Don't lose your balance."

Amanda laughed. "You probably didn't know that Brooke and I are on the gymnastics team. I can't imagine that either of us would lose our balance."

"Well, just don't try any backflips up there," Eddie teased.

It was actually rather pleasant working on the ground level. And even better working in a peace zone. By noon I wondered why we hadn't thought of this armistice sooner. Also, the mural was starting to look pretty good.

"I'll bet we can finish it by the end of the day," I said as we reconvened after lunch. Then, feeling unexpectedly generous, I offered to take everyone out for pizza after the mural was completed.

"Sounds like a plan," Eddie said as he took a bucket of peacock blue up the ladder.

"And I remembered what the rainbow is a symbol of," added Dominic.

"What's that?"

"It's a symbol of hope and promise."

"That's cool," I said. "Maybe the kids will feel hopeful when they see it."

We continued to work quietly through the warm, muggy afternoon, listening to the music coming from the iPod Dominic had hooked up to a speaker. And although it was unfamiliar to me since it seemed to be Christian, it was actually pretty cool. Marissa and I were just finishing up a large section when we heard a scream from above. We looked over in time to see that Amanda had stepped from the scaffolding onto the ladder without considering that Brooke, on the opposite end of the board, had been caught off balance. By the time we got to her, she was flat on her back on the pavement, covered from head to toe in lime green paint. Her eyes were closed, and she wasn't moving.

"Are you okay?" I cried out. "Someone call 911."

She opened her eyes, wiped the paint from her face, and looked up with a stunned expression. "What happened?"

"Are you okay?" I asked again.

"I'm not sure." Brooke tried to sit up, but Marissa stopped her.

"Don't move. You might have broken something."

"That's right," Dominic said. "Stay still." He was off his ladder and at her side now. And Eddie, still up high, was on his cell phone.

"Oh, Brooke," Amanda cried as she came over to join us, "I'm so sorry."

"What happened?" Brooke said again.

"Friday the thirteenth," Marissa said in a serious tone.

Okay, in light of the near tragedy, that comment wasn't too funny. But we soon discovered that Brooke seemed to be fine. Even before the ambulance arrived, and despite our warnings, she was up and walking about and acting like it was no big deal. And even though she looked a little odd in her green coat of paint, the paramedics proclaimed her fit enough not to need a transport to the ER, but they did make her promise to call her doctor for a follow-up consultation. Thirty minutes later her mom showed to pick up both Brooke and Amanda.

"What about pizza?" Brooke called as she paused by her mom's car.

"What?" I'd totally forgotten about my promise.

"Remember, to celebrate getting the wall done?"

"Oh yeah." I glanced back at Dominic and Marissa. "You guys still want to do that?"

"Maybe we should plan it for tomorrow," suggested Dominic, "in case we have to work late to finish this."

"Yeah, that sounds good." I relayed this idea back to Brooke.

She and Amanda agreed to this. And then our labor forces, now down to four, continued to work. Before the day ended, we were visited by the local newspaper, which I suspected was my uncle's doing since he's the editor and knew what I'd been up to this week. Anyway, the four of us posed for some photos, and not long afterward Mrs. Albert and some of her colleagues came down to check on our progress.

"Well, I'm very impressed," she said as they looked on with approval. "This is much nicer than I expected."

It was close to eight by the time we finished. But as we stepped back to look at the completed mural, I was stunned at how amazing it looked. Oh, maybe it was due to the light, since the sun was low in the sky, but it really looked incredible. The color shapes seemed to glow, and the rainbow sprang to life.

"Wow," Marissa said. "It's a lot better than I expected too."

"It's like...magical," Eddie said.

"And kind of spiritual too," Dominic added.

"And it makes me feel hopeful." I sighed. Maybe this really was a sign of things to come.

"So..." Marissa rubbed her hands together like she was about to tell us some grand idea. "Who wants to party?"

"Party?" I glanced at her. "What do you mean?"

"I mean there's supposed to be a great party down at the lake tonight."

"Do you mean that keg party?" asked Dominic.

"Yeah, you guys want to come? The more the merrier."

"Sure," Eddie said eagerly.

I glanced at Dominic, worried that he was going to say yes too. But he just shook his head. "No thanks."

"Count me out," I told Marissa, hoping she might take a hint and think twice about this stupid idea herself. I mean, had she forgotten her dad was a cop? Or was she just determined to push the envelope so far that she'd be kicked out of her house for good?

She frowned at me. "Come on, party pooper. All work and no play makes Maya a really dull girl."

"Thanks, but no thanks. Do you mind dropping me at home before you go partying?"

Now Eddie looked disappointed. "So you guys really aren't going to this thing?"

"If you're smart, you won't go either," Dominic told him.

I frowned at Marissa. "And you shouldn't either."

She just shrugged. "I don't see why not."

"Because…" I glanced at the guys, unsure how much to say. "What about your dad?"

"Hey, it's no secret," she told them. "My dad's a cop, and I got busted with booze in my car."

"And you're still driving?" Eddie looked partly surprised and partly impressed.

"I didn't get a DUI. I don't do *that*."

"How can you say that?" I asked. "If you're driving to a keg party, how do you expect to get home?"

"I don't drink that much, Maya. I'll have a beer or two and just hang and have fun. I'm not stupid. I know my limit."

"Well, those lake parties get busted about half the time," Dominic pointed out. "Even if you're not overdoing, you'll get caught for an MIP."

"Won't be the first time." Marissa just shrugged.

"Oh, Marissa." I shook my head. "I thought you were smarter than that."

"And I thought you were cooler than this. I thought the preaching ended when Brooke and Amanda left." Then, as if to drive this home, she let out a colorful swearword. I was unimpressed. My own mother can do way better than that.

"Here's a solution," Eddie said eagerly. "I'll go with Marissa, and Dominic can give Maya a ride home. That way we'll all be happy."

Okay, I have to admit that I didn't mind the idea of Dominic driving me home, but I was still concerned about Marissa. "Why do you have to go? Why put yourself in that situation? There are other ways to have fun."

"Don't be such a buzzkill. I've worked hard this week. I've been a good girl. It's my chance to have a little fun, okay?"

"It's *not* okay," I said. "But it's not like I can stop you either. Just be careful, *okay*?" Then, to my surprise, I actually hugged her. "It'd be nice if you stayed out of trouble this summer. Maybe we could do something besides community service together."

"This was community service?" Eddie asked with a confused expression.

I laughed. "Yeah, for *some* people!"

"Look at it this way," Dominic said. "If you guys get busted tonight, maybe you can convince the court that you did your community service in advance, Eddie."

Eddie frowned. But that didn't stop him. He just waved us off like we were the crazy ones. Whatever. "See you around," he called as he followed Marissa. Naturally, this left Dominic and me to clean up the painting stuff and put the ladders away. Not that I minded that much. It was kind of cool to be alone with him. Although the youth center was starting to crawl with kids as we piled empty cans into the Dumpster.

"What's going on tonight?" I asked Dominic as we carried the last ladder down the back set of stairs.

"They have dances for middle-school kids. Every other Friday night. A way to keep kids off the streets and out of trouble."

"That's cool." We set the ladder with the others. "Too bad they don't do something like that for high-school kids—keep them from going to the lake to get wasted."

"You really think high-school kids would come to something like this?"

I considered this. "Yeah, maybe not." The truth is, I probably would. I mean, it's like I've missed out on all that kind of stuff. And although it seems nerdy, I think it might be kind of fun. Not that I'd admit that to anyone.

"I used to come to these gigs back in middle school," he admitted. "It was kind of cool at first. But after a while, it seemed like the girls only wanted to hook up with a boyfriend. I wasn't into that."

"Meaning you're not into girls?" I asked with surprise.

He laughed. "No. Meaning I didn't want a girlfriend in middle school. It seemed dumb. I'd see my buddies with their little girlfriends acting like they were so mature, but they just seemed like little kids playing grownups—and not doing it all that well.

Everyone always seemed to be getting upset and hurt and breaking up and getting back together. I just wasn't into all that drama."

"Sounds like you were a pretty smart kid."

"The girls didn't necessarily think so."

Now I laughed. "No. Probably not."

"So what were you like in middle school?" he asked as we
walked toward the dusky parking lot. I paused for one last look
at the mural, but the rainbow looked darker now. Not enough
light to bring it to life.

"I was pretty average." Okay, I had no idea why I said that, but
I wasn't about to tell him what my life had really been like. How
I'd been stuck in a school with a bunch of spoiled rich kids, how
I'd tried to fit in while my addict mom did all she could to ruin
my life, or how I eventually quit public school to do homeschool
simply to avoid the humiliation of having a dysfunctional parent
who had no intention of parenting.

"I can't imagine you being average at anything, Maya."

I glanced at him, unsure what he meant by that. "I guess I'll
take that as a compliment?"

"Yeah. That's what it was."

"Thanks."

"So how's your walk with the Lord going?" he asked as he
led the way through the parking lot.

"Is this your car?" I asked when he stopped by a blue Toyota
Prius.

"Pretty much. I mean, it's not all paid for yet. But I have the keys."

"Wow."

"Is that an impressed *wow*?" He looked somewhat skeptical.

"Absolutely."

He smiled as he opened the door for me. "The last girl who took a ride in it called it a clown car."

"A clown car? That's pretty rude. Didn't she know what a hybrid is?"

"Apparently not."

"How's the mileage? I mean, for real."

"It averages in the midforties."

"Cool."

"So you're really into this kind of thing?"

"You have no idea." I patted the dashboard like I was patting a good dog.

He chuckled as he started the engine. "So...you want to grab a bite to eat before I take you home? I'm starving."

"Sure. But I should warn you that I'm a vegan."

He let out a low whistle. "Vegan?"

"Yeah, is that a problem?"

"Not for me. But it could be for you."

"Why's that?"

"Well, if you've been a vegan for long, you obviously know that eating at a restaurant can be tricky. I mean, I used to be a pretty strict vegetarian, and even that could be—"

"*Used* to be?"

"Yeah, I had some health problems related to lack of animal protein. So I eventually went back to eating eggs and dairy, and now I eat fish and poultry too."

"Oh..."

"Does that offend you?"

"No, of course not. Does it offend you that I'm vegan?"

"Not at all. It's just that I think you need to be careful..."

I was trying not to feel defensive, but I've been down this road before. "I assume you mean careful, nutritionally speaking?"

"Yes. It's not that I want to preach at you, Maya. But I think God would rather have you obey Him than be ruled by your convictions."

"My convictions?"

There was a long, slightly uncomfortable pause now. "Okay, why did you become a vegan, Maya?"

I considered this, then nodded. "I think I get you. I suppose it was because of my convictions against cruelty to animals. But it's also because of my convictions that I've continued being a vegan. What's wrong with that?"

"Here's the deal," he began slowly. "I believe that God cre-ated the earth for us to enjoy and to care for but that we need to keep it in balance. For instance, I realized that being a strict vege-tarian wasn't working for me. I also realized it wasn't something God had put upon me. It was something I'd put on myself. And it turned out that it wasn't healthy for me." He kind of laughed.

"And my poor mom practically lost her mind trying to come up with meals that everyone in our house could and would eat. In other words, my special dietary needs were a pain for others."

"Well, that hasn't really been a problem for me. I mostly take care of my own food."

"And that's cool, Maya. But you need to consider your health too."

"I do."

He was driving in traffic now. "Sorry. I probably came on too strong."

"It's okay. In fact, you could be partially right. I've actually considered giving up the vegan part."

"Really?"

"It's pretty challenging to maintain it, especially now that I don't live within walking distance of a good health-food store."

"So how about dinner? I do know a good vegetarian restaurant. It's a ways away, but they have several pretty good vegan choices on the menu too."

"Sounds awesome."

But once we got there, I decided to step out of my comfort zone by ordering a regular vegetarian dish—an eggplant burrito with real cheese. Dominic tried not to act surprised, but I could tell he was. And when he said a blessing, he specifically asked God to keep me from getting sick after eating something I wasn't used to.

"Thanks," I said after he finished. "But I'm not that worried about getting sick. I've actually eaten cheese a couple of times already. Sometimes Kim cooks dinner, and even though she tries to make it vegetarian, she forgets the nondairy thing. But I go ahead and eat it. I don't want to offend her."

Anyway, I've decided to give this whole dietary thing more thought. Dominic could be right about how I've put this on myself. What if it's not something that God wants for me? I'll admit that it was partly because I care about animals and senseless suffering. But it was also a way for me to take a tiny bit of control over my chaotic life. With my mom and her various addictions, my world was always spinning out of control. Being a vegan was the one thing that Shannon couldn't mess up. It belonged to me—and my crazy mom couldn't take it away from me.

But now I plan to ask God to show me what's best. More than anything I want to live a life where He calls the shots, not me. If that means I need to change some things, then so be it. Although I have to admit that my pride will probably suffer some. Telling people I'm vegan is always kind of fun. In some ways I think it gives me a warped sense of superiority. Probably not that different from how Brooke and Amanda act about religion. And just writing that now makes me want to change!

## Maya's Green Tip for the Day

You don't need to be vegan or even vegetarian to eat healthful foods. But a lot of people are confused about what is or isn't organic. So here are some tips: (1) You can't always trust labeling on packages. Even if it says "natural" or "organic," it might not be. To be sure, look for the USDA organic label. (2) If you buy fresh organic produce that's located next to produce that's been sprayed with pesticides, you may be taking home chemicals that have been spread by the automatic spray system in the grocery store. (3) Most processed foods are not organic. (4) The most important foods to buy organic are dairy, meat, and produce.

# Five

## June 14

Caitlin and I met at the Paradiso Café this morning. To start with, I told her about the completion of the mural project. I also told her a bit about the little "sermons" that Brooke and Amanda seemed to enjoy sharing with the others and how others didn't particularly enjoy hearing them. "It was getting a little combative. Although we did establish an armistice yesterday."

"An armistice?"

"Yes, we declared the work site a no-battle zone." I sighed. "The fighting was really slowing down the mural."

"I see…" Caitlin pushed a silky strand of blond hair behind her ear and smiled. Not for the first time, I was struck by how attractive she is. Not in that flashy, Hollywood blue-eyed-blonde way, although I think she could pull it off if she wanted to. But Caitlin has a softer, classier, quieter kind of prettiness. She just seems to radiate an honest sort of beauty. I suspect it comes from within.

So then I told her how Brooke fell off the ladder and coated herself in lime green paint and how we called 911. Caitlin's eyes got wide with concern, and I hurried to the end of the story.

"Fortunately, Brooke was just fine. She got up and walked around, and the paramedics didn't even make her go to the ER."

"Oh, that's a relief."

"Of course Marissa had to remind Brooke that it *was* Friday the thirteenth."

Caitlin laughed so hard that she almost choked on her latte.

"Anyway, all that interaction with Brooke and Amanda has made me question some things." I actually opened up my notebook. Caitlin has encouraged me to keep a notebook for our meetings—for questions or Bible verses or whatever. I glanced down at my rapidly growing list and shook my head. "I have a lot of questions." I held up my list, and Caitlin's eyebrows lifted.

My Questions (as of June 14)
1. Are Christians really supposed to love *everyone*?
2. Why do some Christians seem kind and loving while others seem mean and critical?
3. What does God think about how we eat? Does He have a preference whether we're vegans, vegetarians, or meat eaters?
4. And what about the planet? Surely God must care for the planet since He made it. Shouldn't Christians care a lot? Why don't they?
5. Are Christians supposed to hang with people who aren't Christians? Sometimes I like nonbelievers better.
6. Like Marissa. I want to be her friend. And I almost

wanted to go with her to the keg party last night—just to make sure she got safely home.

"Wow, this is a great list," Caitlin said as she scanned it. "And just so you know, I won't have all the answers. But God does. Do you want to start with the questions that concern you most just in case we run out of time?"

I laid the list on the table and studied it. "Well, the first one seems pretty important. Are Christians supposed to love everyone?"

"That's actually an easy one." Caitlin opened her Bible. "In Mark 12:31, Jesus says, 'Love others as much as you love yourself.'" She smiled. "Doesn't get much clearer than that, does it?"

"That seems pretty straightforward." I wrote down the Bible verse. "And kind of what I expected too."

"Before that verse about loving others, Jesus tells us to love God with all our heart, soul, mind, and strength. Then He says that these are the two most important commandments."

"And I assume when Jesus says others, well, He probably means everyone, right? Not just to love other Christians."

"Absolutely. My Bible is the Contemporary English Version. But in other versions it reads, 'Love your *neighbor* as you love yourself.' You've probably heard that before."

I nodded. "From my grandmother."

"So a religious guy asked Jesus to define the word *neighbor*, and Jesus told a parable to explain. Have you heard of the good Samaritan?"

"Yeah, I kind of remember that from my grandmother too. Although I don't recall what the story meant specifically."

"Well, it's in Luke chapter 10. It's a story about this guy who's been mugged and left for dead. And when some religious Jewish guys see him on the side of the road, they don't even stop to help."

"Real nice." I shook my head. "And yet they were supposed to be religious?"

"Exactly—that's Jesus's point. So this Samaritan guy comes along. And you need to get that the Jewish people felt superior to the Samaritans, and they put them down on a regular basis."

"But the Samaritan helps the hurt dude, right?"

"Yes. And Jesus used that story to show what it means to be a neighbor. The Samaritan, even though he's been put down, turns out to be the good neighbor."

Now I was trying to wrap my head around this, which led me straight to my next question. "Okay, if Christians are supposed to love everyone, why do some Christians treat some people poorly? Why do some act like they're better than others? Why do some Christians hurt others?"

Caitlin grew thoughtful. "Just because we're Christians doesn't mean we're perfect, Maya."

"I know, but some Christians aren't as nice as some people who aren't Christians."

"You mean the girls who helped with the mural, right?"

"Well, I didn't want to get specific. But I guess I already let that cat out of the bag."

"My best answer is that some Christians aren't very mature in their faith."

"Then why do they go around preaching at everyone else? Why do they act like they know it all and anyone who doesn't agree with them is a stupid sinner?"

"Sometimes it seems that the Christians with the smallest faith have the biggest mouths."

"But that's so wrong."

Caitlin gave me a half smile. "Sad, isn't it?"

"It's even worse than sad. I mean, here I am with Marissa and some others, and we're just trying to get this mural done, and these two heartless Christian girls are dogging on us and arguing with us and making everyone miserable. Why is that? And how is it okay?"

"Like I told you, I don't have all the answers. But I will tell you this. Brooke has gone to church most of her life. But it's only been recently that she started coming to youth group again. And I think she's trying to make up for lost time."

"How's that?"

"Oh, it's hard to explain. But ever since Brooke and Amanda went on a weekend camping retreat and Amanda made her first commitment to Christ...well, I think Brooke feels responsible, like she had something to do with Amanda becoming a Christian.

And now she's on some kind of crusade." Caitlin laughed uncomfortably. "If you know anything about history, you know the real Crusades got a little bloody."

I nodded, taking this in. "So what do you do? What can you say when people like Brooke and Amanda act like that?"

"I try to speak the truth..." Caitlin sighed. "In love."

"But how? How is that even possible?" Then before she could answer, I laid my cards on the table. "I mean, you talk about the Crusades being bloody. Well, the truth is, there were a couple of times I wanted to smack both Brooke and Amanda. I am not a violent person. I don't even eat animal products. But those girls made me so mad, I felt like I could've shed some blood. At times I think I hated them both. To be honest, I wasn't that sad when Brooke fell off the ladder. Oh, when it first happened, I was worried she'd been hurt. But when we knew she was okay, I thought she kind of deserved it. I didn't show it, but I was glad when they both left."

Caitlin didn't say anything, and I was pretty certain she was ready to give up on me completely. In fact, I was ready to give up on me too. I was ashamed for confessing to all that. And yet it was the truth. The ugly truth.

"Seriously," I said, "what kind of Christian does that make me?"

"A human one."

"But you said that we're supposed to love everyone. And that everyone is our neighbor. But I didn't feel any love toward

Brooke and Amanda. I like Marissa more than them, and she's not even a Christian."

Caitlin slowly nodded. "I have a hard time loving some Christians too."

"You do?" Now this caught me totally off guard. "But you come across as the most loving person I know. You're like the perfect Christian."

She laughed. "Then you don't know me well enough."

"But I've seen you at youth group. You are sweet and kind to everyone—even kids who are totally obnoxious."

"Then it's God in me."

"But how?"

Caitlin flipped to another part of her Bible. "Second Corinthians 12:9 is one of my favorite promises. You want to hear it?"

"Sure." I wrote this reference in my notebook too.

"Okay, this is like Jesus speaking to us. '"My kindness is all you need. My power is strongest when you are weak." So if Christ keeps giving me his power, I will gladly brag about how weak I am.'" She looked up at me. "That's how God works. When we come to Him with our inability to do something—like being kind or loving when we don't feel like it—He can help us do it with His power."

"But what if I really don't want to be loving? Okay, I'm trying to be honest here, and it's not going to sound very nice. But what if I really didn't give a flying fig about Brooke and Amanda? What if I just wanted them to go away and leave me alone?"

"Well, that's always our choice, Maya. God won't force us to do anything. He wants us to come to Him for help. But He's not going to shove it down our throats." She closed her Bible. "But you know what I think?"

"What?"

"I think you didn't like that about yourself. I think that's why we're talking about it now."

I considered this. "I suppose that's true. I mean, I want to be a good Christian. I want to care about people. And I suppose I want to love everyone. At least a part of me does. Another part of me gets fed up."

"That's understandable. If it's any consolation, Jesus got fed up too."

"Huh?"

"Jesus stood up against a lot of the religious leaders of His day. He called them hypocrites and snakes."

"Really?" Now this surprised me. Not that I claim to know a lot about Jesus or Bible history. But I did not know this.

"Absolutely. Jesus had zero tolerance for the leaders who used religion to beat people up. He knew that kind of religion only separated people from God."

"So what about religious people who do that now? People who call themselves Christians? How does Jesus feel about that?"

"It must make Him truly sad."

Then instead of focusing on Brooke and Amanda, I focused on myself. "So if I don't allow Jesus to love others through me,"—

I paused to really consider my words—"then I probably make Him sad too."

Caitlin smiled. "Yes, but if you can admit to it, like you just did, there's still hope."

"I guess I really do want Jesus to help me love everyone."

"And maybe Jesus is going to use you to help girls like...well, like Brooke and Amanda."

I couldn't help but wince at this. "Yeah, maybe..."

"And maybe Marissa too."

Okay, that was a little more encouraging.

"I'm worried about her." So I told Caitlin about Marissa going to that stupid drinking party last night.

Caitlin nodded sadly. "Those lake parties have been going on for years. I could tell you lots of stories about kids who got hurt up there."

"I almost wanted to go with her. Just to help her stay out of trouble." I frowned. "Do you think that would've been wrong? I mean, since I'm a Christian and it was a drinking party?"

"My first reaction is to say yes. That's because I wouldn't want to see you in a bad situation. But there are some questions without real black-and-white answers. That's why we need to keep going to God on a daily, if not hourly, basis. Sometimes He might show you that it's right to do a certain thing. Yet another time He might show you just the opposite. If we don't stay tuned in to Him, we could become like those stodgy old religious people who relied on their made-up rules rather than God's leading."

That reminded me of Brooke and Amanda, but I didn't say so. I'd probably dissed those two enough for one day. Okay, more than enough.

Of course we had run out of time by then. I was partly disappointed since I had more questions but partly relieved because that was a lot to take in. Fortunately, I had taken notes and had written down those Bible references. I thanked Caitlin for meeting with me. "I know I've got a lot to learn. I'm glad you're patient."

She just laughed. "Hey, I love meeting with girls like you, Maya. You've got a whole lot more going on than you realize."

"How's that?"

"You seem genuinely hungry for God." She nodded. "Nothing beats that."

Of course, her "hungry" comment made me realize it was almost noon and I really was hungry, which reminded me of my third question on the list, one that would have to wait until next week—vegan versus vegetarian versus meat eater. Which is right? Or does it even matter? Or maybe, like Dominic had recommended, I just need to approach God directly on this one.

So as I left the Paradiso, I shot up a quick "Show me the way" kind of prayer. And it seemed God led me. Or maybe it was my stomach doing the leading. I'm not sure. But as I walked down the street, I smelled something delicious coming from the little pizzeria a few doors down, so I went inside.

That's when I realized I was actually craving cheese. Go figure!

So I ordered a green tea and an enormous slice of cheese pizza and snarfed down the whole thing. I think that settled it. Bye-bye, vegan. Hello, vegetarian. As far as meat goes…I don't think so.

And here's the honest-to-goodness truth: I don't feel the least bit guilty about making this change. I still have a real sense of peace. I think that might be God's way of saying I'm on track.

## Maya's Green Tip for the Day

Where do old sneakers go to die? Unfortunately, most of them end up in landfills, where they might take hundreds of years to decompose. But there's another way out. Nike has a program called Reuse-A-Shoe that recycles old athletic shoes (even if they're not Nikes). Most Nike stores have collection barrels for old tennis shoes, or you can collect them yourself and send them to the address below. But here's what's very cool. The recyclable parts of the shoes (rubber, foam, and fabric) are chopped up into a material called Nike Grind that's used for kids' playground surfacing. And that's way better than piling them up in landfills.

Nike Recycling Center
c/o Reuse-A-Shoe
26755 SW 95th Ave.
Wilsonville, OR 97070

## Six

**June 14, p.m.**

This afternoon I decided to get a summer job, and I plan to begin picking up applications on Monday. Not so much because I need the money. My dad's concert tour continues to be successful, and as a result he has been generous. He sends my uncle "more than enough" to cover my living expenses while I stay here. Plus, he sends me an additional thousand bucks a month. Okay, I think he's trying to make up for something—maybe a lot of somethings—but, hey, that's fine with me. It's not like I plan to send the money back.

And with my mom safely tucked away in prison (doing her time for various convictions on illegal drug charges), I've managed to accrue a nice little pile of savings. Oh, it doesn't equal what dear sweet Mom stole from me last summer. Shannon emptied out the account where I'd stockpiled my emancipation money—the funds I had planned to use to get free of her. But at least I've made a start.

Not that I'm obsessing over my emancipation plan so much these days. I mean, more than anything, I'd just like to experience a "normal" life. If that's even possible. I'd like to be a normal teenage girl, with normal friends, doing normal things. After what I've lived through the past several years, BORING sounds perfectly delightful to me.

Of course, boring is probably one of those subjective things, sort of in the eyes of the beholder. For instance, I like to go out to where Aunt Patricia (that's Kim's mom, who died more than a year ago) had her garden. I've been trying to get everything back to how nice it must've been when she was alive and healthy. Because I love gardens, and I can be perfectly content out there for hours—just pulling weeds, working in compost, staking tomato plants, or watching a bumblebee fly. Nat (who lives next door) thinks I'm insane. But to be fair, I think she's insane too.

Anyway, I haven't completely given up on being emancipated. Although I try not to think about it, since it usually stirs up stressful memories about how dysfunctional life used to be. I so don't want to go back to that. Just the thought of being stuck with Shannon again is horrifying. I'd rather be locked up in prison. At least you'd know what to expect there.

And Shannon plans to appeal her sentencing. At first I thought no way would they let her out. But when I hear something on the news, like how a rapist was released, I get frightened. Not because I'm scared of the rapist. I'm afraid that my mom might be let out. What if she won her appeal? Shannon clean and sober can be very persuasive. And what if she went to court and demanded that I be returned to live with her? In my absence she might convince a judge that daughters are supposed to be with their mothers. Seriously, stranger things have happened—even in my life. I think that perhaps the best thing would be to free myself of Shannon before she gets another chance to turn my world upside down. I mean, I'm still only sixteen. Sixteen going on thirty.

So I've decided to find a job, get my driver's license, and eventually buy a car. In other words, I'll get my ducks in a row and set myself up to be a free woman. Because it's occurred to me that Kim is going away to college in a few months. And my uncle, although a truly sweet man, might want some independence. I mean, he's been through a lot, dealing with his wife's illness, then losing her, raising his own teenage daughter, then taking in his crazy sister-in-law's teenage daughter. He might want a life of his own by next fall. Not that I get in his way or make myself a nuisance. At least I try not to. But who knows? He might want to sell this house and buy a sailboat and see the world. Or maybe he'd like to buy a condo in Florida. In fact, his mother lives down there. And a brother too, I think Kim said.

Anyway, I've decided to do all I can to be independent. I already have my GED, and according to my PSAT scores, I shouldn't have any difficulty getting into college. And here is where I pause and let out a long, loud, tired sigh. The truth is, I'm not sure I'm ready for all that just yet. I still long to be a normal teenage girl. But I need to be strong. I need to be ready to stand on my own two feet. So I will bite the bullet and just do this. And to that end,

I asked Uncle Allen to take me to the DMV (when convenient) so I can take my driver's test. He suggested Monday afternoon. I can't wait.

Okay, enough about me. Oh yeah, this is my diary, and I'm supposed to write about myself. But I have something else to write about—something I'm trying not to obsess over, but it is bugging me. Earlier today I tried to set up a time to take the mural paint crew out for pizza. This sounds easier than it was.

I called Marissa first, but she was too sleepy to talk. "Whatever," she muttered. "Just let me know." Then she hung up. But at least she'd made it home safely after that stupid drinking party. She apparently didn't end up spending the night in the drunk tank or juvenile detention or whatever they do with minors who break the rules. That was something. Next I called Dominic, and he reminded me that it was youth group night. So we agreed to do pizza before that. He suggested we try a new place not far from the church. "It's called Vittorio's," he told me. "But I'm not sure they'll have anything vegan." I assured him that was okay. Then he offered me a ride. And I accepted.

Next I called Brooke. Rather, I called her home since I didn't have her cell phone number. Not that I'd asked. Of course, she hadn't offered it either. But I found what I assumed was her number in the book, then braced myself as the phone rang. A woman answered—I assumed her mom. But when I asked for Brooke, I was informed that she was unable to come to the phone and that she'd been injured in an accident.

"Oh, I'm sorry. Is she okay?" As I said this, I suddenly felt guilty for all the bad feelings I've had toward Brooke.

"We're not sure yet."

"Well, tell her I'll be, uh, praying for her." It felt slightly strange to say that. Being a Christian is still kind of new to me, but I've heard others say that. And I did intend to pray for her.

"Thank you. We appreciate that. May I tell her who called?"

So I gave her my name, and suddenly the woman's voice got very crisp and chilly, like maybe Brooke had told her something bad about me, which wouldn't be surprising. Before I could find out more about Brooke, the woman thanked me for calling and hung up.

As it turned out, neither Brooke nor Amanda came to our little pizza celebration. But both Jake and Spencer, although they had worked less than two days, were happy to come. Marissa arrived about fifteen minutes late.

"It's about time," said Eddie. "We've been waiting for you to get here so we could order."

Marissa grinned down at our group, already seated in the large round booth in the corner. "Maya and four guys... Interesting four-to-one ratio."

"Two to one now that you're here," I pointed out.

"Does that mean we're being snubbed by the little preacher girls?"

"Brooke's been in some kind of an accident." I handed her the menu.

"Did a house fall on her?" Marissa chuckled as she looked over the pizza choices.

"Huh?" Jake looked confused.

"You know," Marissa said, "like the witch in Oz."

Some of the guys laughed at Marissa's joke, but I was relieved to see that Dominic wasn't one of them. "Well, I hope she's okay. That girl seems a little accident prone," he said.

Marissa tossed the menu back at me. "I pretty much like anything on pizza. Other than that kind with pineapple and ham. Yuck. That's disgusting."

Marissa followed me up to the counter, waiting as I placed an order for two giant pizzas and a variety of toppings. "Was it a car wreck?" Marissa asked with mild interest.

I turned and looked at her. "What?"

"Brooke. Was she in a car wreck?"

"I don't know. Her mom didn't say. She actually didn't seem to like me much."

"And that surprises you?"

"Well...I don't really know her."

"Think about it, Maya. Like my grandma says, the apple never falls far from the tree."

I kind of laughed. "My grandma used to say the same thing."

She nudged me and smirked. "See, we are a lot alike, you and me."

I waited for her to order her soda. "You know, you're the one I was worried might get into a car accident last night."

She rolled her eyes. "Me? No way. I'm very careful in my car."

I decided not to push it. After all, we were here to celebrate.

"So did you guys see the photo in today's paper?" I asked them.

"My dad showed it to me," Marissa said. "That probably helped me avoid consequences for getting home past curfew last night." She laughed. "He was actually rather proud of his messed-up daughter for a change."

"We drove by on our way here," Jake said, "to have a look at the mural. It turned out surprisingly cool."

"Meaning you thought it wouldn't?" I asked defensively.

"It was hard to tell."

"Yeah," Spencer agreed. "When we left, it looked like a paint truck had exploded."

"Because it wasn't finished."

"Well, here's to a completed project." Marissa held her soda glass up in a toast. "And here's to Maya's vision for a really cool rainbow."

"Thanks." I was surprised by this compliment. Still, it was nice.

We ate and joked, and finally it was time to split for youth group. Dominic and I invited everyone to come with us, but Marissa quickly declined, and Eddie opted to catch a ride with her instead of being stuck going to youth group. I could tell Dominic was disappointed. And Jake, who sometimes goes to youth group, had been talked into seeing a movie with Spencer instead. So it was just Dominic and me heading over to the church.

We were a few minutes late, and youth group was smaller than usual. But Josh and Caitlin, as usual, were there in front. It's always fun to see the two of them together. They're such an attractive couple. I've heard Kim compare them to a young version of Matt Damon and Gwyneth Paltrow (not that those two celebs are a couple, but the Millers are definitely a striking pair). Anyway, Josh had just started the worship time, but when he saw Dominic, he enticed him to come up and play guitar since the regular dude wasn't there. I didn't even know that Dominic played. But to my surprise, he agreed to help out. And when he did, he was pretty good.

And Josh's message was pretty good too. In fact, I wondered if Caitlin had told him about our conversation this morning, because it seemed like he was hitting pretty hard on religious people who were hypocritical. But maybe it was a coincidence. Unfortunately, neither Brooke nor Amanda was there to hear it. Maybe someone taped it and they could get a copy later. Yeah, right.

During refreshment time Caitlin came over with a concerned expression. "I'm sure you must've heard the news by now."

"What news?"

"About Brooke."

I nodded. "Oh yeah...I heard she was in an accident. Was it a car wreck or some—"

"I thought you knew." Caitlin looked confused. "Didn't you tell me she fell off the scaffolding and—"

"But that was yesterday. And she was perfectly fine. She didn't even want to—"

"Apparently she wasn't perfectly fine."

"Really?"

"According to her dad, she has a spinal injury."

My hand flew to my mouth. "Seriously? Oh no—that's terrible." Okay, part of me was shocked and concerned, but another part didn't get it. How does someone get up and walk around with a spinal injury? And she was definitely walking around.

"That's not all, Maya."

I frowned. "Something worse than that? Did she break something else?"

"No. Not that kind of worse." Now Caitlin lowered her voice. "Her dad plans to file a wrongful-injury claim."

"You mean he's going to sue someone?"

"I'm afraid so." Caitlin glanced around. "I'm not really supposed to say much, but I think you deserve to hear this. When Mr. Marshall learned that I was the one who had suggested Brooke and Amanda help out with the mural, he said he considered suing the church and me as well."

"Oh no!"

"But for some reason he decided to focus primarily on the parks and recreation for his lawsuit."

"That doesn't seem fair."

"No, it doesn't. But he claims they were negligent. He says kids shouldn't have been climbing around on rickety ladders and scaffolding like that. He thinks it was a disaster just waiting to happen."

I considered this. "I suppose that could be true. But isn't that kind of like life? I mean, anyone can get hurt doing anything. I could trip going down the steps coming into the youth group room. But I wouldn't sue anyone over something like that."

"Of course you wouldn't." Caitlin frowned.

"What's wrong with Brooke's dad anyway?"

"There's something else you should know, Maya."

"What?"

"Mr. Marshall informed me that he plans to list you as a responsible party in the lawsuit as well."

"Me?" I blinked. "A responsible party?" I'm barely responsible for myself. How could I be responsible for anyone else?

"Brooke told him you were the one in charge of the project."

"Me? In charge?" I shook my head. "That's ridiculous."

"Maybe so. I mean, I think the whole thing is ridiculous. But Mr. Marshall is an attorney. He thinks it makes perfect sense. After all, litigation and lawsuits are his business."

"Business must not be so good."

She shrugged. "I don't know what to say."

"Well, it seems like a pretty nasty sort of business, going around suing innocent people just because your own daughter is a klutz."

Caitlin put a hand on my shoulder. "Don't worry, Maya. I

doubt that a court could hold you responsible. You're a minor, and it wasn't your fault."

"I'm surprised it's legal to sue a minor."

"That's just what I said. But apparently it is legal."

I was still trying to grasp all this, wondering what I was supposed to do. "So do you think it's for sure? He's really going to sue me?"

"I think it's a possibility, Maya. I tried to talk him out of it. Honestly, the whole thing is just absurd."

"It might be absurd, but it still hurts." I glanced around the room full of "fellow" Christians and suddenly wondered if someone else in this group might do something to hurt me. "I just don't get this. It's like I keep getting blindsided by what Christians are capable of doing to each other. What about that 'loving others' scripture. What about helping your neighbors?"

"I was wondering the same thing, Maya." Caitlin shook her head and glanced over at Josh, who was looking our way with a compassionate expression. "If it's any consolation, Josh feels exactly the same as I do. It's so wrong. I think he and Pastor Berringer will have a talk with Mr. Marshall, and maybe they can reason with him. After all, the Bible says it's wrong for Christians to take Christians to court."

"Really?"

She nodded. "So don't worry about it, Maya. I just wanted to give you a heads-up, you know, in case you hear something through the grapevine. But don't take it too seriously. Not yet anyway."

"Thanks. I appreciate it." Still, I felt like a balloon that someone had slipped a pin into. I mean, I had been feeling enthused about the mural and how cool it looked, how we all had worked together to accomplish it. And now this.

My final conclusion is that I need to get a job. I need to become independent as soon as possible. No way do I want my uncle and cousin to get pulled into my personal dramas. Am I a magnet for trouble? Will I ever escape the craziness that seems to attach itself to my life? Maybe there's an invisible sticker on my forehead (invisible to me anyway), sort of like the Statue of Liberty. And my sticker says bring your troubles, heartaches, and craziness to this girl—she's used to it!

## Maya's Green Tip for the Day

Sometimes a good distraction from troubles is to create something. And maybe you need a new piece of art for your bedroom. But how about making it from recycled materials? Here's how you start. Look around your home (garages are good) for pieces of junk that are just cluttering up space. Then put your scavenged pieces together and look at them differently. Hold them upside down or sideways. Imagine them painted a totally unexpected color and glued or nailed or wired together in a pleasing shape. It can be a sculpture or a wall hanging or something useful like a candleholder or a jewelry rack. Let your creativity go, and see what you come up with. Then you have the satisfaction of transforming trash into treasure.

# Seven

## June 17

As I leaned against the counter watching Kim pore over her open cookbook tonight, it occurred to me that, for cousins, we look nothing alike. Kim is petite and delicate. And even for an Asian, her skin tone is light and creamy. On the other hand, I am tall and bronze and anything but delicate. And my brunette hair is long and wild and curly, while Kim's is sleek, shiny, and black, cut into neat layers that frame her face. The only thing that might be considered somewhat similar is our dark eyes...although I'd like to think our hearts are similar too.

"Don't let her get to you," Kim said suddenly.

"Who?" I set aside my mental comparisons and tried to figure out what she was talking about.

"Dad told me about Brooke." Kim shook her head with an ironic smile. "By the way, congratulations on getting your license."

"Thanks. He told you about the lawsuit?"

"Yeah. I can't believe it." She stretched to open the cupboard overhead.

"I hadn't really meant to tell him," I admitted.

"He was glad you did." She handed me the dinner plates for the table. "Really, sometimes we worry about you, Maya. You keep so much to yourself. And we're your family. Remember?"

"I know, and I appreciate it. I just don't want to dump all my junk on you."

"All your junk?" Kim laughed.

"Well, I seem to be stuck in the land of dysfunction. It's like no matter what I do, I can't escape it."

"Considering all you've been through, you seem to have both feet on the ground. I actually think you're doing really well. So does Dad."

"Really?" I finished gathering silverware, then went into the dining room. And I can't even explain it now, but what Kim said meant so much to me that I actually got a little teary as I set the table. Of course, I hid my emotion when I returned to the kitchen.

"So how's the job hunt going?" she asked.

"Not so great." I didn't admit that I'd been to about thirty different places in the past couple of days, and all I got was "We're not hiring now" or "Go ahead and fill out an application if you like, and we'll keep it on file."

"I've heard it's a tough job market out there. But don't give up, Maya. At least you have experience, right?"

"Yes…not that it's relevant to anything I've applied for." I shook my head. "The only places where they'd even take applications were the yogurt shop and a cheesy jewelry kiosk at the mall."

"Maybe you should set your sights higher."

"Like?"

Kim's brow creased as she sliced a tomato. "Well, you did some modeling last summer, right?"

I frowned. "Not that I'm proud of that."

"And didn't you work at a couple of clothing shops?"

"Not for very long." I rinsed the lettuce and began tearing leaves into bite-size pieces for salad.

"But on Rodeo Drive, no less."

I shrugged. "Not that it's worth much here. I mean, I'm not putting this town down, but it's like another universe compared to Beverly Hills." I smiled. "A very cool universe, I might add."

"But we do have a few sort of fashionable shops here. Have you applied to them?"

"Well, no..."

"Why not?"

I considered this. "Probably a couple of reasons."

"You don't really want a job?"

"No, that's not it." Okay, I didn't admit that the fashion industry isn't my first choice. Although I really wanted to work in a resale clothing store called Second Chances, not that they were hiring or even interested in me. "But if I can't get hired to sell cheap earrings, how would I ever have a chance at some fancy chichi boutique?"

Kim firmly shook her head. "Maya, you are so wrong. If you went in and told them about your modeling and about working

at Ralph Lauren in Beverly Hills…and if you dressed up a little,"
—she frowned at my overalls—"I'm sure you'd have a job in no
time."

"You really think so?" I glanced at the calendar on the fridge
and felt nervous. Summer feels like it's going by quickly. By the
time I land a job, if I even can, I might have only a couple of
months to make enough money to buy a car.

"I'm willing to bet you'll be hired by this time next week."
She pointed to June 24.

"I'm not so sure. But how about if we make the bet worth-
while? I'll bet I don't have a job by then, and my wager will be
fixing dinners and doing cleanup for a week. At least that will
give you a break, and I won't have much to do since I'll probably still be unemployed."

"You're on." Kim grinned. "But not vegan, right?"

"Like I told you, I'm changing my ways. And I'd be willing
to cook chicken or fish too. But I might not want to eat it."

"You're on."

"I'll have to start studying some of your cookbooks."

"But here's the deal," Kim said quickly. "You have to go to the
list of stores that you and I will put together tonight. And don't
ask them if they're taking applications. You have to go in looking
totally cool. You act friendly and confident, and then you hand
them your résumé complete with Ralph Lauren and the modeling agency as references, including the appropriate names and
phone numbers."

"Really?"

"Absolutely."

"Is that how you got your job?" Kim landed a very cool and well-paying job at the Allegro School of Music. She's giving private violin lessons to elementary-school kids all summer.

"No. That was a case of who you know."

"Well, I don't know anyone."

"Not necessarily." Kim smiled like she had a secret.

So after dinner, Kim and I sat down at her computer. She helped me create a résumé, and then she pulled up a list of store names. "The owners of some of these shops were some of my mom's clients. She was their accountant, and they liked her. Anyway, I'm sure when they learn that you're Patricia Peterson's niece, which you will tell them, they will be willing to—at least—give you the time of day."

"I don't want to use your mother's—"

"Do you know how happy my mom would be to know that she helped you—even in a very small way?"

I sighed.

"Seriously, Maya. Can't you just give it a try?"

Okay, although I'm desperate to land a job, the idea of working in the fashion industry again, well, it's a little dismaying...and unsettling. Still, it beats flipping burgers. It might even be better than pumping yogurt, which could've been my best chance at employment. I mean, it's one thing to go back to eating dairy; it's another thing to come home from work smelling like one! So I guess I'll give Kim's plan a try. How can I not? I'm sure it would hurt her feelings if I didn't.

Okay, I have another incentive. And it's not an honorable one. But I can admit this to my diary. After putting together Kim's get-Maya-a-job plan, we were out on the porch enjoying the sunset and some iced tea when Natalie came over. Naturally, Kim told her about my job hunt and her plan to get me hired.

Nat frowned at my faded overalls and just shook her head. "Oh, I don't think Maya could possibly get hired at a place like Divine Diva or Jacqueline's or even Nolita's, Kim. They're way too exclusive for someone like…well, Maya."

And it was as if she'd thrown down the gauntlet. Oh, I kept my cool and acted like her words didn't sting a little. But suddenly I couldn't wait to get dressed up, get on the bus, and go get a job. Well, that's what I'm hoping. But that's probably my pride speaking, and that's not good. I'm definitely going to pray about this job thing. The truth is, I don't want to work anywhere that God isn't leading me.

Naturally, after pointing out that I didn't have a chance of getting a job that had anything to do with fashion, Natalie went on to tell us that Brooke Marshall's lawsuit was becoming the talk of the town. I wanted to ask why that was. Don't people have better things to talk about? But instead I excused myself. For one thing I can't bear to think about Brooke. It's like she's the enemy and I hate her. I hate her moneygrubbing father and her snooty mother too. And I know it's not Christian to hate others—and that makes me feel guilty. But it's the truth. I just don't want to talk about it. Not to anyone. I can barely admit it to myself. But there, it's in my diary now. I hate Brooke and her family!

Anyway, I don't want to think about Brooke right now. Instead I want to focus on getting a job. If I'm going to land a job in some chic shop, I have work to do, including a manicure, pedicure, exfoliating, and all the other little tricks I learned at Montgomery's Modeling Agency last summer. For Kim's sake (and perhaps for Natalie's too) and maybe even for my own, I plan to do all I can to land a job ASAP. When I go in with my résumé, I plan to look like a million bucks. Or at least a few thousand. Thankfully, one of Dad's friends went to our old house before it went into foreclosure and packed and shipped my things to me. (Okay, some of them were originally Shannon's, but she doesn't need them in the pen, and they'd have been thrown out anyway.) I actually have a fairly decent wardrobe to choose from. They might be "second season" in Beverly Hills, but my guess is that they're "cutting-edge cool" here. And I will work them.

## June 20

I know two wrongs don't make a right, but if two rights could fix a wrong, I'd be feeling good right now. As it is, although I'm somewhat encouraged, the black cloud (Brooke Marshall) is still hanging over me.

Anyway, here are the two good things that happened to me today. (1) I was offered a job at Jacqueline's Boutique this morning, and (2) my dad called Uncle Allen and told him that he wanted to buy me a car and asked if my uncle could help me find a good one. My dad wants to buy me a car!!! I'm stunned. Now I'm sure a lot of families out there would assume something like this was just normal. And maybe it is—for some kids. But remember me? I'm the girl who's been dying to try on normal. I'm the girl who wants to live in the Land of Boring. Like, hey, this is the life!

And, okay, it's not like my dad is going to fly home from Frankfurt to go car shopping with me. But at least he wants to help out. I e-mailed him the day I'd gotten my driver's license to tell him the good news. And I hadn't hinted about wanting a car or looking for a job or emancipation or anything. It was just a "hey, how ya doing" kind of e-mail. I thought he'd appreciate hearing how I'd passed my driving test with no problem. Naturally, I didn't confess to the test dude that I'd been driving for quite some time now or that I'd chauffeured my addict mom around in order to be safe. I have a feeling that wouldn't have impressed him much.

Anyway, you could've knocked me over when Uncle Allen told me about Dad's call. And Uncle Allen even offered to help me look. At first I thought it was because he was relieved that I would be more independent and that I wouldn't ask to use his car (which I would never do!). But then I could sort of tell he wanted to go car shopping. Later on, Kim told me that her dad totally loves cars and shopping for them—and if I didn't include him, it would break his heart. So I told him I really needed his help and I wanted to get something with good fuel economy and low emissions that's environmentally friendly. In other words, I want a green car. And if it's green in color, well, that's cool too.

And Uncle Allen told me he was going to do some research. Okay, I didn't have the heart to tell him that I've already done the research, and I'm leaning toward a Prius, like Dominic, although I don't want to look like a copycat. I figure, hey, let my uncle have some fun. And who knows, maybe he'll come up with something totally new and groovy. Anyway, the plan is to go tomorrow. I cannot wait!

Of course, right after Uncle Allen told me about Dad's phone call and the car, he handed me a yellow envelope. "Sorry to be the bearer of bad news," he said. That's when I noticed the name on the return address label: Prichart, Marshall, and Stockton, Attorneys at Law. I vaguely wondered if they'd ever noticed that their initials are PMS? That's about how grouchy they made me feel too!

"But don't take it to heart," my uncle said quickly. "This thing is going to blow over in no time. No judges in their right minds would take this seriously." He lowered his voice now, like someone was listening, although no one was. "I wouldn't want you to repeat this, but I happen to know that law firm has a bit of a reputation."

"A reputation?"

"I'm not tossing this around lightly, Maya, but in my office, they are known as ambulance chasers." He shook his head. "They go after some of the craziest cases. And I don't think they win too many victories in the courtroom."

"That's good to hear, but it's still pretty unnerving. I mean, I've been through all sorts of crud, but I've never been sued by anyone before. I was surprised to find out that minors could actually be sued."

"I did a little research on that myself. Minors can be sued, but they aren't allowed to represent themselves in court. If you don't have a lawyer, the court will appoint a guardian ad litem."

"What's that?"

"Basically an attorney to represent you."

"Oh..." I was trying to act cool about this, like I wasn't as upset as I was feeling. After all, it's not my uncle's problem.

"Can I ask you something, Maya?"

"What?"

"Does Brooke know anything about your father? I mean, that he's, well, rather famous? And fairly wealthy?"

I considered this. "As a matter of fact, that kind of slipped out. Marissa was the one to bring it up."

Uncle Allen nodded. "Well, I'm not saying that's why you're being sued, but I've been a newspaper man for years, and you get a sense about these things. And again, don't repeat this, but the word on the street is that Marshall's law firm isn't doing too well. I've heard they have financial troubles over there. I won't go into details, but this might just be one more desperate move on Marshall's part."

"That is so low!"

He nodded. "I know. I hate to even mention it. Except that you're my niece, and I'm watching your back. I'll do all I can to help you. I've still got some nosing around to do."

Okay, that almost made me break into tears right there in the kitchen. It was so sweet of Uncle Allen. But I managed to control myself. I'm really, really trying to act like a grownup about this stupid lawsuit. I don't want to be a burden. But, honestly, sometimes I just want to be a great big baby and bawl my head off. *Grow up, Maya!*

So I went to my room and opened the envelope and attempted to decipher the legal papers. I swear lawyers must go to college just to learn how to write things up in such a way that no one can understand what they're saying. It took me three times reading through to finally make sense of it. And my IQ was high enough to get me into the gifted program, even if it was in grade school. Point being, I'm not stupid. But even after I translated the letter into understandable language, it still didn't make complete sense. Not the kind of sense that a sensible person would have anyway.

I'd already e-mailed my dad about my latest challenge, telling him that it might blow over but to be prepared just in case it didn't. So he sent me the name and fax number of his attorney in

L.A. I didn't waste any time getting these papers faxed. And now I'm trying to forget about it. Except that every time I see that big yellow envelope sitting on the bureau, it seems to be yelling, "Hey, look at me. Pay attention to me. I'm big and mean, and I plan to destroy you!" Okay, that's a dramatization, but it's how I feel.

Still, I'm trying to focus on the positives. I am going car shopping with Uncle Allen and Kim tomorrow (she wants in on the act too). And I'll begin my new job on Monday, working for the woman who impressed me the most. Her name is really Jacqueline, but she goes by Jackie. And she was a good friend of my aunt. But she seemed to like me—for myself. So really, other than this lawsuit mess, life is good.

# Maya's Green Tip for the Day

It's not easy to understand the latest eco-options in cars. So here are some pointers. A hybrid (like a Prius) is a self-charging, low-emission car that combines a gasoline engine with electric power to increase mileage. Alternative fuels are renewable resources like corn ethanol or vegetable oils combined with mineral fuels like gas, diesel, or even natural gas. Hydrogen fuel cells (still in development) use an electrochemical reaction, and the "exhaust" is simply $H_2O$. Electric plug-in or hybrid plug-in simply means your car must be recharged by connecting to a household current. But that uses up electricity. What I'm looking forward to is all-electric cars that will have solar batteries that can be recharged from the sun. Cool, huh?

# Eight

## June 22

I feel perfectly miserable today. I know I should feel happy—I got a car yesterday. Okay, I wish I could've found something even better than a Toyota Prius (for greenness), but in this town it was the best we could do. For all I know it's the best we can do anywhere. And really, that's not why I'm bummed. I totally love my new car. It's silver and sweet and gets awesome gas mileage and has low emissions. And thanks to Dad, it's paid for. I mean, totally paid for. I had no idea that he planned to pay for the whole thing. I figured I'd have to chip in. But like I said, I think he's making up for some old things. Oh, well. The only fly in the ointment (as far as my car goes) is that I don't want Dominic to think I'm a copycat. Especially because I've admired the Prius since it first came out. It even won Green Car of the Year not long ago. Still, that is not why I'm miserable.

In fact, I was totally euphoric after we got my car. A car that, I'm happy to say, Uncle Allen and Kim both enthusiastically endorsed. Kim said it was like a miracle because we'd been looking for hours, and none of the lots seemed to have any, and then the last place we went just happened to get one in. It had been ordered, and then the buyer changed his mind. I say, too bad for that dude. So anyway, I was feeling pretty great as I drove Kim and myself home. We had the satellite radio on, and we were singing along, and I thought this was how life should be!

To make life even sweeter, I offered to drive to youth group last night. Of course, that meant Nat was going with us too. But I thought, oh well, now she'll hear about the great job I got. Which she did. And she was properly shocked and maybe even a little bit jealous since she works at the same mall but in one of those cheesy stores where only grandmas shop. But I just acted like no big deal. And she didn't say much. So maybe the rest of my evening was one of those things…the pride-comes-before-a-fall kind of thing. I'm not sure. Looking back, I think that might be what happened.

So why am I miserable? Here's how it went down. I parked my car safely away from other cars since I didn't want any door bumps, and we went inside and headed downstairs for youth group. The first person I saw was Brooke, and she was coming out of the elevator, which no one uses except for the handicapped. That's when I saw she looked seriously bad. I mean really, really terrible. Like she'd been run over by a semitruck or thrown under a train. She had this big neck brace attached to some kind of corset-looking thing around her middle, and she was using a walker contraption to slowly get around.

Amanda was with her, and suddenly everyone else gathered around her, helping her and acting very concerned. Then she noticed me and got this terrified expression, like she thought I would come over there and knock her down or break her legs or something horrible. Naturally, I kept my distance.

But the whole time I felt like a piece of doggy-doo stuck to someone's shoe. Unwanted and despicable. And like I better get out of this place ASAP. What made me think I belonged here in the first place? What made me think I could ever fit in with normal? Was this normal?

I was about to take off but then remembered I had brought Kim and Nat. Did I just dump them here? Worship was beginning, and Dominic was helping Josh with music again. Kim and Nat were talking to Caitlin, and I was standing alone and could feel others glancing at me. Their glances felt accusatory—like everyone had heard about Mr. Marshall's lawsuit and assumed I was personally responsible for Brooke's condition. Like I was up there on the ladder and had pushed her off just for spite. Anyway, I just couldn't take it anymore.

So in the middle of worship time, I tossed Kim a look that I hoped she understood, and then I slipped out the back. I went outside to my car, but before I left the parking lot, I texted Kim, telling her I'd be back to pick them up afterward. That's all I said.

To my relief, Kim called me later and said that she and Nat were catching a ride with someone else. I wanted to ask her if anyone noticed I'd left. How self-centered was that? I guess I didn't want everyone to think I was out joyriding in my new car. Although I doubt anyone missed me anyway. But I missed them.

I missed hearing the message at youth group too. And part of me wonders why I didn't stick around. Why didn't I say something to Brooke? I could've shown some sympathy. But that look she gave me—combined with the letter her dad sent me—well, it was just overwhelming.

And then this morning, instead of going to church as usual, I told Kim I didn't feel well, and she and Uncle Allen went without me. The truth is, I don't feel so great. Oh, I'm okay physically. But emotionally...well, I feel kind of broken. I have this ache inside me. Like, once again, my life doesn't work. I don't fit in. Will I ever?

But even worse is that I feel like a complete fraud. I thought I was a Christian. I thought I was learning to love others. I felt hopeful. But this whole thing with Brooke seems to reveal who I really am. Selfish. Hateful. Spiteful. Mean. Hypocritical. False. I didn't believe that she was really hurt. I had been feeling bad toward her and only thinking of myself. And here she is practically crippled. What is wrong with me?

## June 25

This is my third day working at Jacqueline's, and I think it's going pretty well. It's a lot better than I expected and much less stressful than working on Rodeo Drive last summer. Jackie Bernard, my boss and the owner of the boutique, is pretty laid-back. She reminds me of Bette Midler, except that Jackie's a brunette. But her voice, the way she laughs, and even her face all remind me of Bette. And so far, she's been in a good mood. Although today she caught me off guard when she asked if I was happy working for her.

"Happy?" I said with surprise. "Sure. It's great." Okay, *great* was a bit of an overstatement, but it's not bad. Besides, what else do you say to your boss?

She nodded and just studied me. "You seem a little down."

"I'm sorry," I said quickly. "Should I smile more or be more friendly or something?"

She laughed. "No. But if there was anything wrong, I'd want you to tell me."

"No. Nothing is wrong." But since the shop was void of customers, I told her I was feeling a little bummed over the lawsuit, and when she asked for details, I filled her in.

She just shook her head. "Wow, that would be depressing."

"But I'll try not to bring it to work with me," I assured her as I straightened a stack of T-shirts.

"I can't imagine a court would take such a suit seriously. But just in case, do you have an attorney?"

I explained about my dad's lawyer. "Although his expertise is entertainment," I admitted, "he's looking over the paperwork for me."

"An entertainment attorney?"

I could tell she was curious. So I told her about my dad, and as it turned out, she was a big fan. "So your mother is Patricia's sister, and she was married to Nick Stark?"

"That's right."

"I can't believe Patricia never mentioned this." She frowned. "And we were very good friends."

"She didn't know about it...not until shortly before she died."

"Oh..."

So without telling everything, I mentioned how my mother has had some problems. "She ran away from home as a teen, so she was pretty much off the radar with her family. In fact, if Kim hadn't hunted down my mom online when Aunt Patricia got sick, we never would've connected. As it was, we got here too late for me to actually meet my aunt."

Jackie smiled sadly. "Well, Patricia was a truly wonderful person, Maya. I'm sure you would've liked her."

"I feel the same way." Then I told Jackie about working in my aunt's garden and how it makes me feel close to her. "It feels like a real connection."

"I'm not surprised. Your aunt loved to garden."

Then a customer came in, and I was relieved to end the conversation. Not that I don't like Jackie—I really do. But talking about my aunt seemed to be making us both a little blue. Anyway, I did try to smile more and be more friendly and cheerful. I'd hate to think my presence in her shop was bringing people down. And for some reason, we had a lot of shoppers this afternoon, and they were actually buying, not just looking. I think Jackie was pleased, and I actually felt somewhat useful. Then at the end of my shift, Jackie took me aside again.

"Look," she said quietly since a couple of customers were

browsing through the dress rack. "My husband is an attorney, and if you feel you need someone local for your case, I think he might be willing to help out."

I thanked her, and to my surprise, she hugged me.

"I think your aunt would be proud of you, Maya."

I thanked her again, then got my bag and left. And as I drove home in my new car, feeling rather good about my new job, I was almost happy. Except for the dark cloud that won't go away. Cloud Brooke.

## June 26

When I got home from work this evening, I was surprised to find Dominic's car parked in front of my house. Okay, I call it "my" house, but it's really my uncle's house. And Kim's. Still, it feels more like home to me than anything I've experienced in years. And I suppose that worries me a little.

Anyway, Dominic was sitting on the porch talking to Kim and Natalie. I was still dressed for work and, if I do say so myself, looking pretty good. Okay, in that weird fashion way that's not really my thing, but I can do it if I have to. And Jackie really seems to appreciate it. "You bring such a flair to our shop," she told me the other day. "Business seems to be picking up just because you're here." As a result, I take care to look my best.

Of course, it was kind of embarrassing when Dominic let out a low whistle as I walked up to the house. "I'll bet you're whistling at my car," I teased as I paused on the steps.

"No, that was strictly for you." Dominic grinned.

"You clean up pretty good," Natalie said with a slight frown.

I laughed. "Thanks, I guess."

"So how's the new job going?" Natalie peered curiously at me, like she still couldn't believe I'd landed this great job.

"It's okay." This time I was playing it down.

"Any chance you'll get fired anytime soon?" Natalie punched Kim in the arm as if it were all her fault. "I didn't even know they were looking for someone at Jacqueline's, or I might've tried for the job myself."

Kim ignored Natalie's jab as she pointed toward the street, where the two Priuses were parked. "Your cars look like a matched set. Well, except for the colors."

"I hope you don't mind." I turned to Dominic. "But like I told you, I'd always wanted a Prius. And you can't beat the mileage."

"Hey, I think it's cool."

"So how's the lawsuit going?" Natalie asked. And maybe I was just ultrasensitive, but it seemed like she was trying to take another poke at me.

"I don't really know. But my boss's husband has offered to represent me."

"Robert Bernard?" asked Nat in surprise.

I nodded.

"You should be in good hands," Kim assured me. "He's about the best attorney in town."

"That's what your dad said too."

"The whole thing is so ridiculous," Dominic said. "And I'm happy to be a witness. I saw Brooke walking around after she fell. She said she was fine."

"Marissa offered to be a witness too," I told him.

"And I know Eddie would testify for you. He couldn't believe Brooke was pulling a stunt like this. Unfortunately, in Eddie's mind it's just one more strike against Christians."

I nodded sadly. "That's kind of how Marissa felt too."

"Christians aren't perfect," Natalie said, "just forgiven."

"Is that a Bible verse?" I asked.

"No, I read it on a bumper sticker."

We laughed, and I thought maybe I'd been too hard on Natalie. I mean, she's not perfect either. But I guess she's trying. And it felt somewhat encouraging to hang with these guys on the front porch. Kind of like I wasn't as much of an outcast as I thought.

"Anyway," Dominic said, "I tried to call your cell phone today, but it seemed to be—"

"Turned off," I finished. "I don't like to leave it on at work."

"Not me," Nat said. "I always keep mine on."

"Well, I feel like I'm there to wait on customers. Besides, my battery doesn't hold a charge that well."

"I wondered if you wanted to do something sometime," Dominic said. "You know, go out or something?" He clearly looked uncomfortable, like maybe he wished he'd kept his mouth closed in front of our little audience.

Nat tossed Kim a catty sort of look, like Dominic and I were planning some big romance, or maybe she thought we were going to elope.

"Sure," I said quickly, mostly because I didn't want to have this conversation in front of spectators. I mean, I may be sixteen, but it's not like I've really dated. This is still new territory for me.

"So how's your work schedule?" he asked hopefully.

"Well, so far I've been doing the noon-to-eight shift. But Jackie told me that I don't have to work late every evening."

"We could catch a late movie tomorrow," he suggested. "Maybe meet at the mall or something."

"Sounds great." I was trying to act like no big deal. Like I'd been dating for ages and wasn't suddenly feeling nervous or questioning my sensibilities for going out with him. I mean, we've had a good friendship, and that's cool. What if dating messes things up? And yet...I couldn't deny that Dominic is a great guy or that he looked especially hot in his black T-shirt and aviator shades.

I had hoped to ask Kim for advice about this once Dominic had gone, but she and Nat suddenly took off—like they thought we wanted to be alone. As a result, I got very nervous and told Dominic that I needed to go in the house and "take care of some stuff." Take care of some stuff? How ridiculous was that? But he was really sweet about it and just said he needed to go too. Then I went inside, and still wearing my nice work clothes, I got the compost bucket from under the sink and took it outside and dumped it into my compost maker by the garden. Like that was the important stuff I needed to take care of!

## Maya's Green Tip for the Day

Here's how I made my own compost bin. Sure, I could've bought one, but why waste money? I reused an old garbage can that my uncle was going to toss. It wasn't in great shape, but the lid was the kind you can lock in place. I punched holes around the bottom of the can for drainage. Then I found some old cement pavers, left over from a path, and I made a platform to keep the compost bin off the ground. I set this up in a corner of the backyard, out of sight but handy to the garden. Next I layered old grass cuttings and newspaper and green debris from the garden (weeds and stuff), and I sprinkled this with water. Then I added the contents of the compost pail. (That's a small lidded bucket kept beneath the kitchen sink, used for disposing of organic table scraps but not meat!) Then when I'm working in the garden, pretty much daily, I put the bin on its side and give it a few rolls. I add more grass cuttings, newspaper, and moisture as needed. And after one month, presto-change-o, I have lovely rich compost to enrich the soil and grow plants with. Aren't nature (and God) amazing!

# Nine

**June 27**

I don't know why I felt so nervous about my "first date." It was actually no big deal. Okay, that's easier to say after it's over with. Earlier today I was a bundle of nerves.

"Are you feeling okay?" Jackie asked after I absent-mindedly hung a dress on the jeans rack.

"Oh." I noticed my mistake and moved the dress.

"Are you worrying about the lawsuit?"

I gave her a sheepish smile, then told her the truth. She laughed but not in a mean way. "Oh, I remember that feeling."

"You do?"

"Yes, that nervous uncertainty, wondering where the relationship was headed and whether I liked the guy more than he liked me or vice versa."

"Actually I've known Dominic for a while," I admitted. "But we've just been friends."

She smiled. "Well, that's the best way to begin any relationship."

So that's what I told myself. Of course I took some time to make sure I looked good before I went out to meet Dominic in the parking lot. We decided to take my car since he wanted to see how it compared to his. And I even let him drive. Not because I think a guy should do the driving but just because I wanted to show off my car. It's a year newer than his and has a few more accessories.

"I wouldn't have gone for all the bells and whistles," I said. "But someone else ordered the car, and I was just lucky they had it."

"Lucky or blessed?" he asked as he handed me back my keys.

"Huh?"

"Well, sometimes we say we're lucky. And maybe that's the case. But I think God sometimes blesses us, and we just pass it off as dumb luck. And that doesn't seem right."

"You know, I don't usually think about God blessing me. I guess I focus more on the negative things that come my way."

Dominic paused in front of the theater and looked into my eyes. "That surprises me, Maya. All I have to do is look at you, and I can see just how blessed you are."

I frowned at him. "How's that?"

"For one thing you're smart. And you're artistic…and interesting. You even care about the environment. On top of all that, you're beautiful. Don't you think those things are blessings?"

I considered this but wasn't sure how to respond without sounding conceited. Although I have to admit it was nice to hear such sweet things.

"Wouldn't you say those are God-given gifts?" Dominic asked as we got into the ticket line.

"Maybe so…" Actually, the more I thought about it, the more I thought maybe he was right. Maybe I am blessed. And really, it seems the worst things in my life usually come from other people. Like my own mother. And more recently from Brooke Marshall. Anyway, I nodded. "I think you're right, Dominic. I am blessed."

"See." He laughed. "And you drive a great car too."

The movie was only so-so, but we had a good time critiquing it over coffee afterward. We both thought that it ended abruptly and that the plot was slightly contrived. But while I thought the actress did a good job, he disagreed.

"I guess it's good we don't agree on everything," I said.

"Yeah, you know what they say about that."

"What?"

"When two people agree about everything, one of them is unnecessary."

I smiled. "I guess. But sometimes I think I'd like to live in a world where people agreed on more things. I don't really like controversy."

"Meaning this thing with Brooke?"

I was also thinking about my mother just then. But I nodded. "It'll all blow over soon."

"How do you know that?"

"Because I was there that day, Maya. Remember? I saw her fall off the scaffolding, and then I saw her get up and walk around."

"I know. But I was doing some research online, and I read that sometimes people do get up and walk around after a spinal injury, and sometimes that makes the prognosis worse."

"Oh..."

"We really should've made her lie still and wait for the ambulance."

"I guess we could've pinned her down." He gave me a half smile.

"I mean, it's not like I think it was my fault. Not really."

"Well, it wasn't."

"But I still feel guilty."

"You shouldn't."

I sighed. "And I feel guilty for having had bad thoughts about her."

"If it makes you feel any better, I've had bad thoughts too."

"But we're supposed to be Christians," I protested. "We're supposed to love everyone."

"Fortunately, God doesn't expect us to become perfect all at once. I suspect it's going to take some time...maybe an entire lifetime." He smiled. "Don't be so hard on yourself."

As I drove Dominic back to the mall to get his car, he asked me about youth group tomorrow night, saying that he'd be playing guitar again. But then I wasn't sure I would be there.

"Because I'm playing guitar?" he teased.

"No, of course not."

"Because of Brooke?"

"She gave me such a weird look that last time I saw her. And I felt so miserable. Just seeing her like that, well, it pretty much took the fun out of being at youth group."

"Maybe it's not supposed to be fun."

"Maybe not..." But even as I said this, I couldn't help but think it wasn't supposed to be torture either.

"But I guess I understand."

By then I was feeling fairly relaxed about the whole dating thing. In fact, I wondered why I'd been so worried. Then I pulled up by his car, and suddenly I wasn't sure what I should do next. It seemed kind of weird to get out of my car, like was I going to walk him to his? So I simply thanked him for the movie and coffee. And okay, it was one of those moments...like is he going to kiss me? Should I lean over and be ready? Am I even ready? Thankfully, before I could do anything stupid, he took my hand. I thought he was going to shake it and say good night, but he lifted it up to his lips and kissed it. Just like that. I sort of giggled then. Yes, giggled. And I am not a giggly girl. But it kind of tickled. Okay, it tickled in a very cool way.

"Thanks for going with me tonight," he said. "And I hope you'll reconsider youth group tomorrow. I could pick you up if you—"

"No thanks. If I go, I want my own wheels."

"So you can make a quick getaway?"

I smiled. "Maybe..."

As I sit in the privacy of my room recording all these private thoughts, I feel kind of tingly and electrified and different inside.

I know it's because I *really* like Dominic. And that kind of scares me. And yet, it's also exciting. The last time I felt anything like this was with Jason, but I think that was infatuation, combined with desperation. And my dad threw a fit when he found out I had a crush on one of his roadies. To be honest, I can see my dad's point now. Oh, Jason was a cool guy and nice—and good-looking. But he was a lot older than I was. Anyway, that was the end of my touring with Dad. Still, this feels different with Dominic. For one thing, he's just a tiny bit older than I am. He's seventeen and will be a senior next year. For another thing, I suspect that he likes me as much as I like him.

But here is my main concern. I don't want my feelings for Dominic to distract me from God. I know that probably sounds weird to some people, but it's true. This thing between God and me is the real deal. And it's important to me. I've never had this kind of peace about my life before. Not since my grandma was alive, and even then, I'm not sure. I doubt if most people (especially ones my age) would get this. But I plan to ask Caitlin for advice when we meet for coffee tomorrow. She's about the most God-conscious person I know.

## June 28

Okay, I didn't ask Caitlin for advice about Dominic this morning. I just couldn't think of a way to say it that didn't sound juvenile and dumb. I mean, one date…he kissed my hand…big deal. Besides, our conversation went down a different road. And not a road I really wanted to take. Caitlin brought up my mom. Very gently, of course—she is, after all, Caitlin.

Besides Uncle Allen and Kim, Caitlin is the only other person in this town who knows about my mom—not only that Shannon is incarcerated but also that she's an addict and has never been much of a mom. About the only thing Caitlin doesn't know about the situation is that I'm still considering being emancipated.

"So how do you deal with your mother?" She looked evenly at me with those clear blue eyes. I always get the feeling that she can see beyond the Maya I try to show most people. And yet it doesn't really bother me. It's good to have at least one person in your life who knows who you really are.

"I don't know…," I told her. And that was an honest answer.

"I was thinking about your situation this week, and I was praying for you…and it just hit me. Like, wow, that must be a really heavy load for you to carry."

"Yeah…"

"And yet you seem so together, Maya. I mean, anyone looking at you would think, *This girl's got it all*. For starters, you're gorgeous. But that's just the surface. You have a great head on your shoulders, and you really care about people. I seriously doubt anyone would begin to guess all that you've been through."

I nodded. "Probably not. And I suppose that's the way I like it."

"I understand. Still, you might need to talk about it sometime. Not necessarily to me, unless you want to. But I've had enough counseling training to know that something that huge has an effect on a person. Whether you're not totally aware of it now or you're just concealing it well, there's a lot of hurt in you, Maya. After what you've endured, it's humanly impossible not to have some pretty deep scars. But I also know that Jesus is making you whole. Still, it might take some time."

Okay, I was about to cry then. I don't know why, but genuine sympathy just gets to me like that. Probably because I'm not that used to it.

"I don't want to make you feel bad," she said quickly. "I just want you to know that I'm here for you. I know that sounds trite, but I mean it. And if you need to talk about how you feel about your mom or things you've been through, the very least I will do is listen. And you know I'm already praying for you."

I nodded again, swallowing against the hard lump in my throat. I took a quick swig of my lukewarm mocha. "Here's the deal." I could hear the husky sound in my voice, and I wanted to say this as quickly as possible. "I know my mom's messed up. And I know she's hurt me. I'm fully aware of these things. But right now…all I want is to live a normal life. That might sound silly, but it's the truth. Do you know what I mean?"

"I do. Totally."

I sighed. "I realize there are things I still need to work out with my mom. Some pretty big things. But I'm not in any big hurry."

She smiled. "You're an amazing girl, Maya Stark."

"What makes you say that?"

"You're so mature and grounded." She paused to think.

"Without naming names, I counsel other girls your age, and they seem so young compared to you. But that has a lot to do with what you've been through. You were forced to grow up early." A look of realization crossed her face. "In fact, you remind me a lot of my best friend."

"Really?"

"Yes. Beanie Jacobs was my best friend in school. Actually, she's still my best friend but from a distance. And seriously, you two are so much alike. I think that's why I was drawn to you in the first place."

"Wow…I'll take that as a compliment."

"Her mom had some problems too." Caitlin shook her head. "You know, I almost forget about it now, because her mom is doing so well."

"That gives a person hope."

"Absolutely. But like you, Beanie grew up fast. Even though we were the same age, I always felt like she was older in some ways."

I nodded. I knew exactly what she meant, only in reverse.

"You'll have to meet Beanie. She's in New York right now. She went to design school there and has been apprenticing at a very impressive studio this past year."

"Very cool."

"Yes, Beanie is very cool. And very talented. She actually designed and made my bridal gown. It was spectacular." Caitlin went on to explain how she'd been worried and how Beanie had waited until the last minute to show her the gown.

"Wow, you must've really trusted her."

"I did, but I was still concerned. You see, Beanie has always loved retro and remaking old clothes—"

"So do I!"

"I know. It's just one more way you two are similar. Anyway, I had to hold my imagination at bay—thinking she'd show up with something she'd reconstructed from her ragbag." Caitlin laughed. "That was not the case. Not at all."

"So what will she do when she finishes her apprenticeship?"

"She wants to have her own design studio. But she wants it to be different from the usual. She wants to design clothes that are"—Caitlin paused as if trying to remember—"you know, ecologically sound and environmentally conscious."

"Yes! Earth-friendly clothes. I totally get it. That is so awesome!"

"Well, you would get Beanie too. And I promise you, when she comes home in the fall, you two will meet."

I realize this is a small thing—well, for some people. But I am so excited to meet this girl. And I can't help feeling even more connected to Caitlin now. I mean, I always liked her, but she is so different from me. And yet her best friend sounds so much like me.

Before we said good-bye, Caitlin asked if I was going to youth group tonight, and I told her I was thinking about it. Naturally, she encouraged me to come and said I shouldn't be concerned about Brooke. She even promised to sit by me, which kind of made me feel good and bad. Good because I like her. Bad because it makes me seem like a sympathy case. I don't need that.

Anyway, later in the day I thought about what we'd talked about. And as I got into my car and drove over to the church, I even prayed about everything as I went. But just as I was about to turn into the parking lot, I saw Brooke being helped out of her mom's car. She still had the walker thing and the braces, and she really looked pitiful. It was more than I could handle, so I just kept driving.

Call me a coward. Or nonconfrontational. Or just a peace-loving earth muffin. But I did not need that tonight. I drove around town for a bit, then came back here, where thankfully no one was home. And I spent the evening putting together a decorative water fountain for the patio. Okay, I was a little lonely. But really, lonely is nothing new to me. Besides that, the fountain turned out to be amazing.

## Maya's Green Tip for the Day

Remember when I told you about "recycled art"? Well, this is how I made a decorative fountain for the patio. First I had to buy a fountain kit at the local hardware store. Then I took an old washtub and treated it with a special kind of paint that made it look even older, kind of rusty but cool. Then I put some large stones in the bottom to anchor the pump. I cut a piece of old screen (probably from a window) into a circle and placed it over the stones and pump, making a hole for a water tube from the fountain. Then I put smaller, prettier stones on top of that, and I stuck in an old decorative garden faucet that had never worked quite right. But it's cute with a frog on it. I pushed the tube right into the bottom of the faucet so that the water would come out the spigot, pouring back into the rocks. And I filled the whole thing with water, plugged it in, and voilà—we have a fountain.

## Ten

**July 1**

U ncle Allen surprised me by showing up at Jacqueline's just in time for my lunch break. (It's actually more like an early dinner break since it's at four.)

"How about if I take my favorite niece out for a late lunch?" He winked at Jackie like she had known he was coming.

I laughed. "Do you have any other nieces?"

He shook his head and smiled sheepishly. "But still."

"Just let me get my purse." Luckily, Marissa wouldn't be meeting me for lunch like she often did. She'd already told me that she was doing community service on a road cleanup crew for the next two weeks, and they were required to eat their lunch alongside the road. And since Dominic had just been by yesterday, I doubted he'd show up again today. Although I had been hoping. Still, I was curious as to what had brought my uncle to the mall.

We settled into a booth at the only restaurant in the mall with waiters to serve, and after we placed our orders, I looked curiously at my uncle. "So did you get off work early?"

"Actually, this is work related."

"Oh? Some big story breaking here at the mall?"

He chuckled. "Not exactly. I've come to proposition you."

My eyebrows lifted, and he laughed.

"I guess I should make myself clearer. Do you remember your challenge to me about the recycling boxes and how our town needs to be more environmentally aware?"

"Of course."

He frowned. "It's not going as well as I'd hoped, and today I got an inspiration."

I nodded, waiting for him to explain.

"This is an idea that involves you, Maya."

"Me?"

"Yes. I wondered if you'd be interested in writing a green column for the paper. We'd publish it in the Twenty Below section."

"Twenty Below?"

"That's a section for young people. It comes out on Saturdays, so you'd only need to write your column weekly. And I don't think it has to be too long, just a way to make readers more environmentally aware. You could share some of your concerns about conservation or recycling or whatever in an attempt to educate the readers. What do you think?"

I wasn't sure what to think. On one hand I was flattered. But at the same time I felt uneasy.

"That seems like a pretty big responsibility. I mean, I'm only sixteen."

He nodded. "If it's any consolation, we've done something

like this before at the paper. We have an advice column called 'Just Ask Jamie.'"

"Yes, I've read it a couple of times, and it's good. Are you saying it's actually written by a teen?"

"That's right. And the teen was about your age when the column began."

"Really?"

"You seem sincere in your quest to protect the planet. And you also seem to know a lot about it. By the way, Kim showed me that patio fountain you made from recycled pieces. It's really delightful."

"Thanks."

"In fact, you might even write in the column about doing something like that."

"I guess…" Still, I wasn't so sure. What if I messed up?

"And I realize the writing part of this might be a challenge to you. Do you like to write, Maya?"

"Actually, I do."

"Great. But if you wanted, we could pair you with an editor, just to help you get started. One thought I had was that the column could simply be suggestions for ways that readers can practice conservation. Sort of how-to tips."

That's when it hit me. "Hey, I've already been writing green tips."

"Really?" He looked surprised. "How is that?"

So I explained about my journal. "I've been doing it for fun. At first I pretended it was part of my homeschooling, but then I just kept doing it."

"Amazing." He grinned. "Looks like I came to the right girl."

"I guess…"

"And this is a paying job."

Just then our food came, but even before the waiter set my veggie burger on the table, I knew I wanted to do the column. "Okay," I told my uncle. "I'd like to give it a try."

"Maybe I could have a look at some of the tips you've already written."

"Sure. But they're not very long. I could probably add to them though."

"Sounds great."

After lunch we shook hands, and I realized that before long, I would be a published author. Who would've thought?

## July 2

This morning Uncle Allen asked if I minded having my picture taken for the column. I just laughed. "Actually, I got pretty used to being photographed last summer." I told him about my short modeling stint. "But I'll admit that when I first started and had to get my portfolio shots taken, it was pretty intimidating."

"Do you still have your portfolio?" Kim filled her dad's coffee mug. "I'd love to see it."

"I almost threw it away." I took some clean plates out of the dishwasher. "But it was kind of expensive to have done, so I saved it."

"Hey, maybe we could use one of those photos," my uncle suggested. "That would save us having to get new ones taken."

So I went to my room and dug out the portfolio. To be honest, I wasn't that thrilled to see it again. But I handed it over to Kim and my uncle, then went back to emptying the dishwasher.

"Wow," Kim said. "These are really great photos, Maya."

Uncle Allen laughed. "Yes, and I'm sure it will get the readers' attention to see such a beautiful young woman who cares about the environment. It's rather unexpected, don't you think?"

"I think Maya's column is going to be a hit," Kim said. "What are you going to call it?"

"I've been trying to think of something clever with the word green in it," he told her. "Do you have any ideas, Maya?"

"Nothing that sounds very interesting."

"I have an idea," Kim said, "although it might sound kind of goofy. Do you remember Kermit the Frog?"

"Of course!" I put the last glass away and closed the cabinet. "I adored Kermit."

"How about 'It's Not Easy Being Green'?"

I considered this, but I wasn't sure. "What if people think it's for little kids? Like the Muppets or something?"

Uncle Allen nodded. "And there could be a problem with copyright."

I put the last dish in the dishwasher and closed the door. "How about…'It's a Green Thing,'" I suggested.

"That's good," said Uncle Allen.

"I like it." Kim nodded.

"It's a Green Thing," Uncle Allen declared. "That works for me." He wrote it down on a notepad, then put one of my publicity headshots next to it.

"Are you sure you want to use that photo? I mean, wouldn't it be better to get a shot of me in my overalls, like in the garden or separating the recyclables in the trash?"

He laughed. "Come to think of it, some shots like that would be fun. Maybe we can do both."

Kim gazed down at the glossy photos on the table. "She's definitely photogenic."

Suddenly I wasn't so sure. "You're not letting me do this just because of that, are you?"

"Of course not, Maya. We know you're sincere about your commitment to the environment."

"That's right," Kim said. "We have to live with you."

I kind of laughed. "I guess it's not easy living with someone who's got a green thing."

"Put like that, it sounds like a disease," teased Kim.

"A disease that is hopefully catching," I shot back.

Although I could joke about it, I'm still a little worried about this column. Uncle Allen is convinced that it's just what young people need, and he thinks it'll be a success, but I'm not so sure.

Last night I showed him several of my green tips, and we finally decided on the one that explains the three Rs—reduce, reuse, recycle. It's actually rather basic and a good place to begin. But that's not what worries me.

What worries me is me. I mean, what if I'm the wrong person to do this column? Just because my uncle runs the newspaper doesn't mean I should have this opportunity. Yes, I definitely care about the environment, and I think people my age should be challenged to think of ways to help. But I'm working in a place that has little to do with environmental concerns. How am I going to feel when someone says, "Oh, there's that girl who acts like she's into conservation, but she works at that chichi boutique. What's up with that?" And really, isn't that sort of hypocritical on my part?

During a lull in the shop this afternoon, I mentioned my worries to Jackie. Naturally, I said it all wrong.

"Are you suggesting my shop is not environmentally sound?"

"No, not at all."

"Because I do care about the environment, Maya. You've noticed that I recycle the cardboard from shipping boxes."

I nodded. "But there are other things you could do."

"Really?"

So I quickly suggested some things she might do to help conserve and protect the environment, and to my surprise she listened and actually took notes. "My goodness, Maya, I had no idea you were such a thoughtful conservationist. I'm very impressed.

No wonder your uncle wants you to write that column for the paper."

"And I can print out some things for you about fair trade and organic cotton and lots of things to do with the fashion industry."

"I'd like that. In fact, Rosemary has been mentioning these very things. I've just been too busy to take notice." Rosemary is Jackie's daughter. She's in her midtwenties and works at the shop occasionally—so far only on days when I wasn't there, so I haven't met her yet.

By the time I left the shop, I was encouraged. Okay, maybe I don't work in a thrift store or a recycling center, but I'm helping my boss do things differently. That's something.

## July 3

"Any big plans for July Fourth?" Marissa asked me today. She'd stopped by unexpectedly for my lunch break. It seemed the road crew boss wanted the day off, and as a result Marissa and I shared a cheese pizza at the food court. I think I may be getting seriously addicted to cheese. I wonder how I ever survived without dairy before.

"Dominic is taking me to the fireworks," I told her as I went for a second piece.

"You guys getting serious?"

I shrugged and wrapped a string of mozzarella around the tip of my slice. "How do you define *serious*?"

"You know, like exclusive, like in love, like you're sleeping together."

I blinked. "No, then I can safely say we're not serious." I don't admit that we haven't even kissed. Well, he did kiss my hand that night, but that's it. Still, I have a feeling that our first kiss isn't too far off. Or maybe I'm just hoping. "How about you?" I asked, eager to deflect the attention. "Are you still seeing Eddie?"

She laughed. "No. That was just a one-night thing. He's fun, but he's too young for me."

"So what are you doing for the Fourth?"

"There's a big party on the far side of the lake. We'll be able to see the fireworks from there but still have a good time."

"A good time?"

"You know." She rolled her eyes as she sipped her soda.

"I just don't get why people think getting drunk is a good time."

She shrugged. "Because you get to let your hair down and unwind."

"Why can't you do that without alcohol?"

"Because that would be boring."

"I don't drink, and I'm not bored."

She seemed to consider this as she reached for another slice.

"Here's the deal, Marissa. I've seen other people—people I know really well—who have ruined their lives with drugs and drinking. I just do not see the attraction. I mean, I never want to end up like that."

"Like what?"

"Like your life is ruined because you did something stupid... like being arrested for underage drinking or using drugs or drunk driving."

"Those things wouldn't necessarily ruin your life."

"But they could," I point out. "And they have ruined some lives."

"Not mine."

"Maybe not completely. But look at you. You're stuck doing community service all summer."

She grimaced. "Don't remind me. It's been less than a week working on the road crew, and already I feel like road kill."

"That's my point. You have to know that it's not worth it to keep making bad choices, Marissa. I just don't understand why you're willing to risk everything."

"Everything?"

"Yes. Like your freedom, for one thing. I mean, you're not exactly free to do what you want when you have to do community service. But seriously, if you got caught again, like tomorrow at the lake, you could end up going to jail."

She grinned. "Yeah."

"Marissa?" I stared at her.

"It might be interesting doing time."

Okay, I was so tempted to tell her about Shannon and how that is not the least bit interesting. But I just couldn't go there.

"Oh, you're such a worrywart, Maya."

"I just care about you. And honestly, I don't get it."

"What's to get?"

"Like I said, why you're willing to take such risks. Don't you care about your life?"

She shrugged. "Maybe I'm just getting even."

"Getting even?"

"With my parents."

I had to think about this one. "You mean because your dad's a cop?"

"Partly. But also because my mom messed up."

Now this was news to me. "Messed up?"

She made a nonchalant face. "Yeah. She cheated on my dad a few years ago. It wrecked their marriage. She left us to be with her lover. She messed up."

"I'm sorry…"

"Hey, that's life. You know what it's like. I mean, your parents are divorced too."

I hadn't actually told her this, but I guess it wasn't hard to figure out. "You're right. But that just proves my point."

"What point?"

"That I don't need to mess up my life just because my parents messed up theirs."

She leaned forward with interest now. "So are you saying your parents messed up too?"

"It's no big secret, Marissa. My parents' marriage was a mess. And although they were both to blame, my mom has probably messed up worse than my dad. And even worse than your mom."

Marissa smiled. "See, I knew we had things in common."

"But still," I persisted, "we don't have drinking and partying in common. You're acting like you do that to get back at your parents, but you're really only hurting yourself."

"I'm not hurting."

"Not now maybe." I sighed. "But it's not like you're enjoying your road crew work. At least you admitted that much."

She smirked as she held out her browned arms. "Hey, it's not all bad. Check out my tan."

"Let me guess...you don't use any sunblock either."

She rolled her eyes. "Okay, Maya. I didn't drive all the way to the mall to get lectured on the dangers of living and breathing. Can you give it a break?"

So I clammed up, and she changed the subject to Brooke's lawsuit, and suddenly I was the one on the hot seat. Finally I told Marissa that I really didn't know how it was going to turn out. "I've been praying about it," I said, "and I'm trying not to obsess over it. My uncle and my attorney both think it's going to blow over."

"Or else there'll be a settlement. I'm sure that's what Brooke's dad is hoping for. He wants to get a piece of Nick Stark's money and keep it out of court."

I nodded. "My attorney said that's a distinct possibility."

"Well, that's so wrong."

"I know."

So I guess we broke even today. I bummed Marissa a little with my lecture, and she got me back by reminding me of Brooke and the stupid lawsuit. I'd actually been doing a fairly good job of blocking that, but now it's haunting me again. And I feel sorry for my dad. I mean, he works hard for his money. Why should he have to pay for something like this? It just makes no sense.

Something else makes no sense. Marissa. I just can't figure her out. So what if her mom messed up? So what if her parents split? How does Marissa putting her own future at risk make anything better? I so don't get that.

## Maya's Green Tip for the Day

I wouldn't tell my uncle this, but I believe newspapers will be obsolete someday. I think everyone will get their news online. In the meantime, if people would simply recycle their newspapers *one time a week,* like on Sunday, those papers could be recycled into 212 million pounds of cellulose insulation. According to *Delta Sky* magazine, that would be enough to insulate 118,767 Habitat for Humanity houses (about twice as many Habitat homes as have been built in the United States now).

## Eleven

## July 4

There were fireworks tonight! And I'm not just talking about the sky, although it was really beautiful to see the explosions reflected on the lake. I tried not to think about the crazy party on the other side of the lake. I just hope that Marissa is okay. I'm praying for her.

But the fireworks I'm talking about are when Dominic kissed me. Yes! We had our first kiss. And second...and third...and so on. And it was totally amazing! I really felt like the earth was spinning and like I was floating and like Dominic and I were the only two people on the planet. Wow.

Still, something about this evening made me uncomfortable. I mean, the kissing really was superb. But afterward, well, there was this uncomfortable silence. Kind of like there was nothing more to say. And one of my favorite things to do with Dominic is to talk. But when the fireworks ended (both the show and the kissing), we were kind of at a loss for words. Then Dominic drove me home, and we kissed again (in the car). Then he walked me to the door, and we both said a kind of stiff good night. And I went to my room and felt uncertain. What if all that kissing messed up what we had going? I mean, I love the idea of having Dominic as my boyfriend. But I also like him as my friend. What if I can't have both?

I'm just not sure. But I do plan to ask Caitlin for advice. We meet again tomorrow. And this time I will speak up. Besides, that might keep us from talking about Shannon. There are two people I just don't want to think about right now—Shannon and Brooke. I suppose that's avoidance on my part, but it's the truth.

Okay, it's tempting to go on and on about Dominic now. To write about how wonderful he is. How much fun it was to kiss him. How I feel like I'm in love. But that all seems kind of juvenile. I never wanted this diary to become like that. And I really, really do not want to be boy crazy. That is so not me.

## July 5

"Here it is." Kim handed me the newspaper this morning. "Your first column, Maya. Doesn't it look great?"

I looked at the Twenty Below section and felt a simultaneous rush of panic and pride. "Wow."

"Look, it's right next to the 'Just Ask Jamie' column."

I nodded and stared at my photo. Even though it was taken a year ago, it makes me look older than I am. It probably makes me look prettier too. "Do you think anyone actually reads this section?" I asked nervously. "I mean, anyone our age?"

Kim laughed. "Well, for the newspaper's sake, let's hope so."

"Hey, it looks like your dad wrote an introduction for my column." I paused to read it, then sighed. "That was sweet."

"He's proud of you, Maya."

I glanced at her. "You're okay with that, right?"

"You mean, am I jealous?"

I barely nodded.

"Of course not. I'm proud of you too, Maya. And if it makes you feel better, my dad is very proud of me too."

"I know."

I read through the column, then handed the paper back to Kim. "I guess that wasn't too bad."

"Not too bad?" She poked me in the arm. "You're a published writer, Maya. Not many teens can say that."

"I guess."

"Don't you want to keep this for your scrapbook?" She handed me the newspaper, and I took it to my room and placed it on my portfolio. I know I should be pleased, but somehow this attention feels a little unnerving. And as I drove to meet with Caitlin, I found myself hoping that no one really reads that part of the newspaper. I've barely read it before. Of course, that will change now that I'm part of it. Still, it's weird knowing that a piece of you is out there for the public to see. Modeling was sort of like that, but there was an anonymity too. It was just my face and my body, not my thoughts or my name. This changes things.

"You're famous." Caitlin held up the newspaper as I sat across from her with my mocha. "I thought you might like an extra copy."

"Thanks." I folded the paper and slid it into my bag, then shook my head. "I don't think I want to be famous."

She chuckled. "Maybe you should've thought of that sooner."

I frowned.

"Don't worry," she said quickly. "I doubt too many people read that section of the paper."

"That's what I was hoping."

"Although that 'Just Ask Jamie' advice column is pretty popular."

To change the subject, I told Caitlin that I had a question about dating. Suddenly she was all ears. So I told her about Dominic and how we've gone out a couple of times.

"He is such a great guy," she said. "I really respect him."

I nodded. "Yes."

"So what's your question, Maya?"

I told her about the fireworks...and kissing. I could feel my cheeks getting hot as I said this. I even glanced around the coffeehouse to make sure no one was listening.

Caitlin just smiled and nodded. "And...you said you had a specific question?"

"Well, afterward...it just seemed so awkward. And I felt uncomfortable. We didn't talk at all. And I just wondered..."

"You wondered if something was wrong?"

"Yes."

Caitlin's expression was thoughtful now. "Has Kim or anyone told you about my personal convictions?"

I shook my head. "No, what do you mean?"

She chuckled. "Well, I have kind of a reputation."

"A reputation?" Somehow this did not seem like the Caitlin I knew.

"For being anti-dating."

"Anti-dating?"

"Yes. When I was in high school, I did the dating thing too. But it just didn't work for me. Dating made me feel that I was being compromised as a Christian. Like the relationships got carried away. Guys always wanted to go farther than I wanted. It was out of my comfort zone."

"So you became anti-dating?"

"I did."

"Wasn't that hard?"

"For me it was easier. It allowed me to be friends with guys without the pressure of getting too physically intimate. And now that I know a little more about guys, I realize that too much intimacy isn't good for them either." She shook her head. "The stories I could tell."

"So is kissing wrong?"

"I can't really say what's right or wrong for you, Maya. I mean, in regard to kissing. But it was wrong for me."

"Then how do I know what's right or wrong? For me."

"You have to ask God to lead you. But I can give you some pointers if you want."

"Sure." I got out my notebook.

"Well, to begin with, God speaks to us with a quiet voice. The Bible calls it a still, small voice. It's like your conscience. The trick is that we have to listen. We have to stay tuned in."

"How?"

"Like I've told you. We need to spend time in God's Word, reading the Bible. And we need to spend time in prayer. And we also need to spend time with other Christians." She looked intently at me now. "We need to be in fellowship, Maya, like youth group and church."

"Meaning I've blown it by skipping youth group?"

"I can't say, but you should ask God about it. That's the tricky thing about being a Christian. God speaks to us individually. That puts the responsibility on us to listen. And if you feel uncomfortable about where things are going with Dominic, well, that might be God speaking to you."

I nodded. I sort of understood. Not completely, but sort of.

"Is Dominic your first boyfriend?"

I wanted to say no, but that would have been a lie. I just nodded again.

"Have you thought about where you stand in regard to sex? I mean, sex outside of marriage?"

I'm sure I looked uncomfortable.

"Do you mind if I speak candidly, Maya?"

"No, that's why I asked you."

"Well, God's best plan for us is to wait until we're married to have sex. How do you feel about that?"

"I think I agree."

She smiled. "But you haven't really thought about it?"

"Oh, sort of. But the opportunity never really presented itself." I shrugged. "Not that it has now. I mean, no way were we going there, Caitlin. We were just kissing."

"I know. But that's always the way it starts. I'm saying this from personal experience. You think it's just about kissing. And maybe it is for you. But guys are wired differently, Maya. Especially at this age. It's like their hormones are totally raging, and sometimes they can barely control themselves."

I glanced around again, worried that someone might be listening. But everyone seemed intent in their own conversations.

"Sorry if I'm making you uncomfortable."

"It's okay. I need to hear this stuff."

She laughed. "You'd be surprised how many girls I've had this exact same conversation with."

"You mean those immature girls?" Suddenly I wished I hadn't brought this up. I liked it better when Caitlin thought I was mature for my age.

"No, I didn't mean that at all. It's an important conversation to have. I'm just saying that I'm kind of used to it now, and I don't mind being honest. That is, if you don't mind."

"No, I don't mind."

"I've seen a lot of Christian girls try to figure out the dating dilemma. What's right? How far is too far? I've seen girls make a sincere commitment to abstain from sex until marriage. And I've seen them blow it. They get caught up in a moment, they feel pressure, they rationalize that they're in love, and suddenly the commitment is tossed by the wayside." She paused to sip her coffee. "And then the girl gets hurt."

"Hurt?"

"Oh, some girls act like it's okay, but I don't buy that. The first thing that gets hurt is their walk with God. And then they usually get hurt by the guy moving on—and that's almost always the case. Then they suffer self-esteem issues. And I've even seen girls who end up pregnant."

"Pregnant?" Okay, by that time I was wishing we weren't having this conversation at all. I mean, I have no intention of getting pregnant.

"You look surprised, but it's a fact of life. What I've seen happen with good Christian girls is that they do not plan to have sex. So then when it happens, they are totally unprepared."

"Meaning birth control?"

"Exactly. Now I'm not saying that they should have a condom in their purse, but on the other hand, they shouldn't think that God will protect them from pregnancy."

"Of course not."

She smiled. "Am I going too far?"

I kind of shrugged.

"I'm only saying all this to point out that it all starts with having a steady boyfriend, Maya. And then kissing. And then the envelope gets pushed a little further. And some couples get carried away. Not all of them. But if you let nature takes its course, well, it usually leads to intercourse."

Still, as she said this, I was thinking that I am different. And Dominic is different. Finally I said as much.

"Everyone is different, Maya. But I doubt that you and Dominic are immune to this. Although I do think it's great that you're considering these things early in your relationship. See, that just shows that you are mature. Sex is something every teenage girl needs to think about and come to grips with. God has a great plan for you, but He can't bring it about if you don't cooperate with Him."

"I want to cooperate."

"Well, dating is probably the number-one way teens get derailed in their relationship with God. There's just no easy way to say it except to say it's a fact."

"So these girls—the ones who blow their commitment not to have sex—do they lose their relationships with God as a result?"

"Some do temporarily. But God is always there, waiting to forgive and to heal. Still, He wants to save us from senseless suffering."

I was sitting there, trying to take this in. I really had a hard time thinking that any of that could happen to me. I'm a sensible person. I don't think I'd let things get that carried away.

"Remember my best friend? The one I told you about last week?"

"Sure. The designer in New York."

"Yes. Beanie Jacobs. She's given me permission to share her story with the girls I counsel. When we were in high school, Beanie and I both made a vow to abstain from sex before marriage. But Beanie started dating this guy, also a Christian, and they got carried away. She broke her vow."

Now this disappointed me. "Beanie?"

"She thought she was in love. And I think because she didn't have a dad, well, she was really looking for a guy to love her in a special way."

"And he did?"

Caitlin sighed. "Not exactly. When Beanie discovered she was pregnant, her boyfriend, Zach, was totally derailed. They broke up. Beanie got her heart broken, and Zach got involved in drugs. It was really sad."

"Oh…" I shook my head. "Beanie got pregnant?"

"She ended up losing the baby. Even that was pretty tragic."

"But she's okay now?"

"Yes, she's doing great, thanks to God's grace." Caitlin smiled. "The only reason I'm telling you about her is because back then I never dreamed that Beanie would do something like that. She was mature in so many ways. I felt totally blindsided by it."

"Are you telling me this because you think it could happen to me?"

"All I'm saying is it can happen to anyone, Maya. And it does."

I looked down at my empty coffee mug.

"Okay, how about we talk about something else?"

I nodded hopefully.

"I'm organizing a benefit concert to raise money to help school kids. It's called the Back-to-School Backpack Project, and the plan is to purchase and fill backpacks for underprivileged kids so they'll feel more confident when they go back to school in September."

"That's very cool."

"Anyway, I'm looking for helpers. I know you're pretty busy, but if you're interested in being on the committee, I'd appreciate it."

So I agreed, and Caitlin explained that the concert will be in early August. And Chloe has agreed to bring Redemption, her band, to play for the event. In the meantime we'll try to get some things donated from various vendors, like door prizes and the printing of tickets and fliers.

"It sounds like a great event," I told Caitlin as we went to our cars.

"I hope so." Caitlin lowered her voice. "And I hope I didn't make you too uncomfortable with my little sex talk, Maya."

"No...I mean, yeah, it was a little uncomfortable. But you've given me a lot to think about."

"Now do you get what I meant when I said I have a reputation?"

I had to laugh. "Maybe so."

I have to admit that Caitlin made some good points. And although I don't think it really applies so much to me, it's nice that she cares. But seriously, I don't think I'd ever let things get that carried away with Dominic. I really don't.

## Maya's Green Tip for the Day

I used to live in a drought area. And although it's not the case now, I have an old habit that's hard to break. You know how you turn the shower on and run it awhile to get the right water temperature? Well, I keep a watering can handy so I can collect this water, which would otherwise be going down the drain. After my shower I use it to water the potted plants on the patio or porch.

# Twelve

## July 10

I didn't work today. Jackie has decided that Thursdays and Sundays will be my official days off. Anyway, I figured it was time to pay Brooke a visit. If I didn't have a private conversation with her, it would continue to be difficult for me to make it to youth group. And like both Caitlin and Dominic have been saying, I need fellowship.

So while puttering around the garden and praying for Brooke this morning (something that Caitlin has recommended I do more often), I decided to pick her a bouquet of flowers—they are at their best right now—and drive over and attempt to have a Christian-to-Christian conversation with her. To say I was nervous is a huge understatement. But the bouquet was gorgeous, and I cleaned myself up and was ready to go and tell her how sorry I was that she'd been injured but also to point out that I didn't think it was really my fault. What could it hurt?

To boost my confidence, I prayed as I drove across town. She lives in an upscale neighborhood on a hill that overlooks the town and the lake. And her house is one of the nicest and nearly on the top of the hill. Still, it probably isn't that much nicer than my parents' home in Beverly Hills. Not that it matters. But I was trying not to feel intimidated as I parked in the circular driveway and walked up to the large brick house. I rang the doorbell and waited, but no one answered. At that point I decided to go back to my car and write a quick note to leave with the flowers. Okay, maybe it was the chicken way out, but there didn't seem to be anyone home. Plus I thought my peace offering might make it easier to have a conversation with Brooke later, perhaps at youth group.

But as I was walking to my car, I heard a screeching yell and a splash from around back—almost as if someone had fallen into a pool. Imagining that Brooke had stumbled with her walker, plunged into a backyard pool, and was now drowning, I dropped the bouquet and sprinted around the side of the house, got a side gate open, and breathlessly ran around to where, sure enough, there was a backyard pool. But to my stunned surprise, Brooke was in a bikini, bouncing on the diving board, and she executed a nearly flawless one-and-a-half flip as she dove into the water.

At the shallow end of the pool was Amanda, gasping with her mouth open and eyes wide as she stared at me walking toward them. I must've looked equally shocked as I stood at the edge of the pool, waiting for Brooke to emerge, which she did, smiling victoriously as she looked at Amanda.

"I think that was a ten—" Then she must've realized Amanda's expression was odd, and she turned around to see me standing there, watching them.

"What is going on here?" I demanded.

"What are you doing here?" Brooke shot back at me. "Breaking and entering?"

"No," I said calmly. "I heard a scream and a splash, and I thought perhaps you'd stumbled with your walker and fallen into the pool. I came back here to help."

"Yeah, right." She shook her head. "You're spying on me."

"Apparently, you need to be spied on." I glanced over to where her walker and braces were on a nearby lounge chair. "Is this some kind of physical therapy?"

"It's none of your business." Brooke climbed out of the pool. "And if you tell anyone, I'll deny it."

"How about you?" I asked Amanda. She still looked shocked. "Would you lie for Brooke? In court?"

Amanda didn't say anything, and as Brooke turned to look at her friend, I slipped my hand into my bag and retrieved my phone. Fortunately it was on. And although I've only taken a couple of photos with it, I somehow managed to aim it and snap a shot as Brooke turned around, glaring at me with hands on hips, dripping wet in her hot pink bikini.

"Give me that." She charged at me.

But I just snapped another one, an action shot, before I quickly made my way out of there.

"You'll be sorry," she screamed. "I'll call the police and tell them you broke in here."

"Go ahead," I shouted back as I retraced my steps through the side yard and out the gate. I scooped up the dropped bouquet.

No way was I wasting my beautiful flowers on that liar! I hopped into my car. My heart was pounding hard as I started the engine. I drove directly to the newspaper building, where I found Uncle Allen in his office and showed him the photos, quickly explaining my surprise visit.

"Well, I'll be!" He shook his head as he looked at the pictures. "Who knew you were a private detective, Maya."

"It was totally accidental. I actually thought she'd fallen into her pool and was drowning. But when I got back there, she was doing a nearly perfect one-and-a-half dive into the pool. She's really good."

He laughed. "What timing!"

I considered this. "You know, I'd been praying all morning, just trying to work up the nerve." Then I told him about the flowers.

"Seems like you did the right thing," he said. "Now let's get these pictures downloaded onto my computer, and I'll shoot them over to Robert Bernard to use as evidence." He chuckled. "I can't wait to hear his reaction."

Before long Uncle Allen had Mr. Bernard on the phone, telling him to check his e-mail. He waited for a bit, grinning at me as he thumped his pencil impatiently. "That's right, Robert. The calendar and clock are accurate. Maya took them less than an hour ago." He nodded. "Yep, right there in the Marshalls' back-yard. Caught the two girls completely by surprise." He laughed. "That's what I told Maya. Guess we should start calling her P.I. Stark."

"So can he use them?" I asked after my uncle hung up. "In court?"

Uncle Allen waved his hand. "Oh, I don't think this will be going to court, Maya."

"Brooke said she was going to call the police on me. She accused me of breaking and entering. But I only went back there because I thought she was in trouble."

"I'll let Robert know about that too, but I doubt it will be much of a problem. Not with these photos." He looked back at his computer screen, then shook his head. "These are pretty incriminating."

I looked at the photo and let out an exasperated sigh. "You know, I should be relieved, but this really makes me mad."

"That's understandable."

"I mean, I can't believe she was faking it!"

"Unfortunately, things like this happen a lot. Not that it makes it any easier to take. The good news is that your ordeal with the Marshalls will soon be over. Be thankful for that."

"I am. But when I think of how horrible I've felt these past few weeks—it just really irks me!"

"Don't let it get to you, Maya. They say the best revenge is living well. So do something fun, and enjoy your day off."

"Okay. I will." I thanked him again.

"Oh yeah," he said before I left. "We're getting good feedback on your column. It seems to have struck a chord with some of our readers."

"Cool."

So as I drove back home, trying to think of something fun to do, I tried to focus on the positives. The lawsuit would soon be history. My column was doing well. Really, life was good. I called Caitlin and told her the news. She was so relieved. Then I called Marissa, and like me, she was incensed that Brooke was such a liar. "Nice Christian girl," she said bitterly.

"Not every Christian is like that," I pointed out. "And maybe she's not really a Christian."

"Yeah. She's probably been faking that too."

"Well, she didn't fake that dive."

Marissa laughed. "I wish I could've been there to see her face."

"I'll send you the photo," I promised. And I did.

Finally I called Dominic. He couldn't believe it. Then he suggested we celebrate by going out, which we did. A jazz band was playing in the park, and we went and picked up Greek food and sat in the park and listened. It should've been a great evening, but I couldn't fully enjoy it. I was still stewing over Brooke.

And even now, it's nearly eleven, and I should probably go to bed, but instead I'm writing in my diary. I still feel angry at Brooke. Instead of going away, my anger seems to be growing. Really, how could she claim to be a Christian and do something so low? I don't get it.

## July 12

Dominic took me to youth group tonight. Almost everyone has heard the truth about Brooke by now. And while part of me feels vindicated, another part feels vindictive. I don't want to admit it to anyone, but I am still angry. And I wasn't a bit surprised that neither she nor Amanda came tonight. The cowards!

"It's too bad Brooke and Amanda didn't come to youth group," Caitlin told me privately.

"Why's that?" Okay, as soon as I said this, I knew it sounded all wrong. Especially considering that Josh's talk tonight was about forgiveness. I'm still chewing on it, but mostly I don't want to think about it.

"I just think that now more than ever Brooke needs good fellowship. She needs to experience forgiveness and see what being a part of the body of Christ is really about. She needs to feel God's love in action."

Unfortunately, I do not feel terribly loving toward Brooke right now. Or Amanda. And I wanted to ask Caitlin whether Brooke should have to come and ask me for that forgiveness first. I mean, was I supposed to just give her the free-and-clear and act like she didn't really hurt me? But it would probably sound petty...and not very Christlike. One of the things Josh said tonight was that we're supposed to forgive the way Jesus did—completely and whether the other person deserves it or not. But how is that done?

I think Brooke should get down on her knees and come crawl-ing to me, saying how sorry she is and begging me to forgive her. And even then, I might have to think about it awhile. Maybe a few weeks...or about the same amount of time that she strung me along with her phony-baloney lawsuit. Because I feel pretty sure that Brooke would've continued her little drama queen act right up to the point when my dad handed her dad a big fat check. And that really burns me. How can I forgive that kind of selfishness? How can I act like it didn't hurt?

Just the same, I'm trying not to obsess over Brooke. I keep reminding myself of what my uncle said: the best revenge is to live well. So I'm trying. And tonight after youth group, Dominic and I took a little moonlight stroll through the park. I wished that Brooke could see me with him, just laughing and enjoying our-selves like normal teens.

The walk seemed like a fun idea. But then we sat on a bench in an isolated section, and before I knew it, we were kissing. Then we were really making out. And okay, it felt really good—tingly and exciting and wonderful. Part of me just wanted to keep kiss-ing Dominic forever. But another part was saying, "Hey, slow it down. Enough is enough."

But did I actually say those words aloud? Of course not. And that has me worried now. Why did I let it just go on and on? Why did Dominic? The worst part is that when we finally pulled away from each other, we both got really quiet. It's like we both knew something was wrong. As we went to the car, he held my hand, but we didn't talk. And as he drove me home, we made small talk and goofy jokes, but it was like we weren't ourselves anymore. Like we'd left something behind in the park. And it really, really bugs me.

Now I'm thinking, *What if Caitlin is right? What if Dominic and I get carried away? What if we end up like Beanie and her boyfriend?* I so don't want to go there. I need to talk to Caitlin again. Did I listen carefully enough the first time? Maybe being normal isn't so fun and easy after all.

## Maya's Green Tip for the Day

"Green is the new black." And lots of Hollywood people are sporting the latest, greatest environmentally conscious designs. But not everyone can afford to buy earth-friendly clothes. And that's when I say hit the thrift stores and secondhand shops. Still, when you need something new and you have the choice, why not buy clothing made from organically grown fibers and other renewable resources? Because the more popular these green lines get, the more reasonable the prices will become, and then everyone will jump on the bandwagon. So be a trendsetter and dress green.

# Thirteen

## July 15

My attorney stopped by the boutique this afternoon. "I've got news for you," he told me. Because we had customers just then, Jackie suggested we go to the back room to talk.

"Did Mr. Marshall settle?" I asked hopefully. Mr. Bernard had sent a letter to Brooke's dad late last week, but Mr. Marshall had been out of town for a few days.

He laughed. "Settle?"

I frowned. "What, then?" Okay, I'm not exactly a legal expert.

"To settle would mean that we pay them to keep the case from going to court. Under these new circumstances, a settlement would be ridiculous. I simply informed Mr. Marshall that we were considering a countersuit for—"

"But I don't want to sue anyone. I just want all this to be over and done—"

"Yes, I realize that, Maya." He smiled patiently. "But you're probably aware that lawyers play games sometimes. I simply wanted to make it clear that the ball is in our court now. And to ensure Mr. Marshall and his daughter understand we are willing to play hardball if necessary."

I sort of laughed. "You're really into sports metaphors."

He grinned. "I'm sure Jackie's told you that I'm a bit of a sports fan—or *fanatic* as she calls it."

"So...what happened?"

"Well, yesterday I received a letter from Mr. Marshall denying the validity of the photos. This didn't surprise me."

"Why?"

"He's an attorney. It was an expected reaction. So your uncle and I met him for coffee this morning."

"Really?" I couldn't imagine Uncle Allen and Mr. Bernard having coffee with Mr. Marshall. Okay, I don't even know Mr. Marshall, but I imagine him as this mean, evil lowlife.

"It was your uncle's idea. At first I wasn't too sure."

"So how did that go?"

"We sat down like civilized gentlemen and showed him copies of the photos and asked him to explain them to us."

"Did he?"

"He actually looked fairly shocked. He studied the copies closely, examined the dates, and made some notes. Finally he just shook his head, and I knew we had him. Just to be certain, I assured him that the photos would stand up in a court of law."

"And?"

"He was rather upset."

"So he didn't know that Brooke was faking it?" Now this just made no sense to me. How was that possible?

"Apparently not. Or else he's a very good actor."

"But what about the doctors, the braces, and all that?"

"Yes. Exactly what we asked Mr. Marshall."

"And?"

"He admitted that Brooke had gotten in trouble with her mother the same afternoon that she fell off the scaffolding."

"In trouble? For falling?"

"No. It seems that Brooke had lied to her mom about using a credit card a couple of weeks ago, and Mrs. Marshall had received the bill that same day. She was not happy."

"Oh?" I sensed where this was going now.

"So Brooke played on her mom's sympathy by allowing the accident to take center stage and distract her from the credit-card bill."

"It was a pretty big fall," I admitted.

"True. And it's possible that Brooke was injured, but not to the degree that she played it up."

"But wouldn't x-rays show that?"

"Spinal injuries are complicated. Every spine is different. And often the doctor can only treat the symptoms." He sighed. "Brooke started complaining of pain and went to lie down. Later on she said that her legs were numb and that she couldn't get out of bed. As you can imagine, her mother was alarmed."

I nodded.

"So she called for paramedics, and Brooke was transported to the hospital, where her drama act took on a life of its own."

"And the credit-card bill was forgotten."

"Naturally."

"Then Brooke was trapped in her lie," I said.

"Exactly."

"So she just kept it going."

"That's what her father is thinking."

"That is so mean."

"And selfish."

Even so, I have to admit I felt a certain amount of relief that it was only Brooke playing this nasty game. Well, Amanda too. But at least her parents weren't in on the scam. It had been pretty disturbing to think Mr. and Mrs. Marshall were that messed up.

"Brooke's dad is probably having a long talk with Brooke right now."

"And the lawsuit?"

"There will be no lawsuit."

"Not on our part either?"

"Not unless you want to—"

"No," I said quickly. "I just want it to end. I mean, I realize you've put time and energy into it, and I know my dad will pay you for whatever you've—"

Mr. Bernard smiled. "Don't worry, Maya. It's not as if I wanted to take Brooke to court. But I do hope she learns a lesson. And I hope her parents don't let her off easily."

I nodded. "Me too."

"I did tell Mr. Marshall that Brooke owed you an apology, and he promised to see that it happens."

I frowned. "A forced apology?"

"Hopefully, she'll be genuinely sorry."

"Hopefully…"

Still, I'm not so sure. She's probably mad that she's been found out and furious at me for catching her on camera. How did she think she could continue her little charade without being discovered? And what a pain it must've been to wear that silly brace and use a walker! A high price to pay for Mommy's pity.

But even more than that, how can Brooke come before God and act like what she did was okay? Didn't she feel like a liar and a hypocrite? I mean, I realize Christians aren't perfect. But what about that still, small voice we're supposed to listen to? Why couldn't Brooke hear it herself? It's just too weird.

## July 17

My dad called this morning. He usually checks in with me about once a week, depending on his schedule. But I'd already called him on Tuesday, leaving a message about the lawsuit. Naturally, he was relieved. But he was also curious about the details, so I explained why Brooke faked the whole thing. And like me, he was astounded.

"Man, that's a pretty hard act to keep up," he said. "And I can't imagine how hot and cumbersome it would be to wear a body brace in July."

I had to laugh. "Maybe that's why she decided to go swimming."

"In a way, being stuck in her medical getup might've been a form of punishment in itself."

"I guess. Although I think she enjoyed the attention it got her." Everyone at youth group had gathered around her, helping her, showing sympathy. And although wearing the brace must have been miserable, I hope her parents dole out a little more punishment.

I still can't believe what she put us all through. Yesterday I added up all the people who were affected by her little scam, and there were more than twenty: my family, people at church, my boss and her husband, the park and recreation people, even Brooke's family—and probably Amanda and her family too. That's just crazy. If I wasn't so selfish about wanting to live a normal life, I might actually consider participating in a class-action suit against Brooke Marshall. Okay, probably not. I remember what Caitlin said about Christians not taking other Christians to court. But…is Brooke really a Christian? I don't think so.

Anyway, the main reason my dad called (besides expressing relief over the lawsuit) was to tell me he's taking a few days off toward the end of July.

"I'd like to come visit you, if that's okay," he told me.

"Yeah, sure…" I knew I didn't sound too excited, and I think he heard the uncertainty in my voice.

"Unless it's not a convenient time for you, Maya. I wouldn't want to be an intrusion or anything—"

"No no," I said quickly. "Really, Dad, it'll be great to see you."

"You're sure?"

"Absolutely."

"Naturally, I'll stay in a hotel. I don't want to put Allen out."

"Yeah. That might be a good idea. This house isn't that big, and I've already taken over their guest room."

"Anyway, I thought you might get a couple of days off from your job, and we could spend some time together. Maybe do something fun. How does that sound?"

"Awesome, Dad."

"And to be honest, I'll probably just need some downtime too. I'm pretty exhausted, and I still have the Scandinavia tour to do. I'm booked ten nights during the next two weeks."

"Wow, that sounds pretty tough," I said. "Make sure you take good care of yourself, Dad."

"Thanks, baby. I appreciate it."

Although I was pretty shocked that my celebrity dad is coming here to Small Town USA—probably making a splashy entrance into my otherwise normal life—I am trying to be okay with it. He's not coming here to be in the limelight. He just wants to see his daughter, and that's nice. And he really sounded tired. He'll need to take it easy. Nick Stark never goes anywhere without being recognized, and that can be a pain. So my plan is to keep everything very low-key.

I told Kim and Uncle Allen about his impending visit, and they both seemed eager to meet him. But I made it clear that we didn't want anyone to make a fuss. "He's looking for some downtime since his concert schedule has been pretty grueling. He'll want to keep a low profile."

"No worries there," Uncle Allen said. "I can understand his desire to fly under the radar."

"Totally," Kim agreed. "But maybe we can barbecue here at the house one evening."

"That's a good idea," I said. "And I want him to see my—I mean, Aunt Patricia's garden."

My uncle smiled. "It's your garden too, Maya. And Patricia is probably smiling down from heaven to see how fantastic it looks now."

Kim nodded. "This is the best it's looked in years."

"And maybe we could invite a few people," I said, suddenly eager for a social event. "Like Jackie and Robert Bernard—they've been so supportive of me."

"I'm sure your dad would like to meet some of your friends," my uncle said, "so he can see what your life is like."

"You're right," I said. "I'll make a short list. And I don't want you guys to lift a finger for this little soiree. I'll handle everything."

"I'm happy to help," Kim said.

"And I'm pretty handy on the barbecue," Uncle Allen added.

"Okay." I nodded. "But I'll be responsible for getting everything together, and I might hire a caterer for some of it."

"This is sounding very cool," Kim said. "I can't wait."

So really, I'm going to be okay with having my dad here— and it'll only be for a few days. Besides, I'm looking forward to seeing him again. I've made out a guestlist that includes the Bernards and Dominic. I might ask Marissa and her dad since he's such a fan. And maybe Caitlin and Josh. But I'll try to keep the number under twenty.

## July 19

I met with Caitlin again this morning, and she asked me about Brooke Marshall. "Have you spoken to her yet?"

I shrugged. "No, why should I?"

She frowned slightly. "I guess I just assumed that you'd want to."

"Why?"

"Well, this is a small town, Maya. And even though you don't see her much during summer break, you will see her at school in the fall. And you might see her at church, if she isn't too embarrassed to show up."

"I didn't see her there on Sunday."

"Exactly. Josh and I were concerned, so we went to visit her this week."

"You went to her house?" Why would they want to go see Brooke Marshall? I actually felt sort of betrayed, like they had suddenly switched sides and were now against me.

"Josh said that if Brooke wasn't going to come to us, we would go to her."

"So...how did it go?"

"Okay." Caitlin smiled. "We called her mother to make sure Brooke would be home. Mrs. Marshall actually seemed glad that we wanted to come visit. She assured us that Brooke would most definitely be home—in fact she will be home for the rest of the summer since that's how long she's grounded for."

I nodded with a smidgen of satisfaction. "I'm glad she has some consequences."

"She has a lot of consequences." Caitlin took a sip of her mocha. "Besides being grounded and responsible for all the household chores—since both her parents work outside the home—she is also one sorry girl."

"Good. She should be." Okay, that came out all wrong, but it wasn't as if I could take it back. "I mean, I'm glad she's sorry."

Caitlin studied me for a moment. "Brooke really regrets what she did, Maya. She said that her back really had been hurting that night. And although she was playing it up for her parents, she went online and read about spinal injuries and actually became somewhat convinced that her fall had been more serious than she'd thought."

"Right…" I could hear the sharp tone of skepticism in my voice, and I didn't like it.

"I know it's probably hard for you to believe, and I'll admit that Josh was a little suspicious, but I can see how that might happen."

"Okay. Let's say that's what happened. But the time had to come when Brooke realized her back was fine. I mean, I saw her doing a nearly perfect one-and-a-half off her diving board. And she came up grinning like that was so great—until she saw me anyway."

"Yes, that's a valid point. And one that Josh brought up."

I nodded, mentally thanking Josh Miller.

"And she admitted she had known for a while that her back was okay, but by then the lawsuit was a big deal, and she was afraid to tell the truth."

"So she just kept on lying?"

"Yes." Caitlin looked sad now. "But I didn't really want to talk about Brooke's problems—and I'll admit she has some. I'm here to talk to you, Maya. I'm concerned that this thing between you and Brooke could turn into a big stumbling block for you."

"How's that?"

"Remember Josh's talk about forgiveness?"

I nodded and looked down at the table.

"Like Josh said, God forgave us everything even when we didn't deserve it, and He expects us to forgive others. When we don't, we construct a barrier that separates us from God. Every day that we remain unforgiving becomes one more brick in that wall. And eventually we can't even see over it."

We talked some more about forgiveness, and while I understand in theory, I'm just not sure how to put it into practice. Caitlin gave me a short list of Bible verses about forgiveness. And I promised her I would read them and pray specifically about this. And I will. But not today. Of course, I've just laid another brick.

Still, that wall can't be too tall yet. I mean, it's only been a little more than a week since I found out Brooke had lied to us. That would only be eight or nine bricks, and that wouldn't be much of a wall. Unless these are very large bricks. But I'll think about this tomorrow.

## Maya's Green Tip for the Day

Do you have a wall wart? That's a recharger stuck in an outlet with nothing to charge on the other end. Or maybe you have an energy vampire. That's an appliance that's plugged in but not in use. Did you know that the U.S. Department of Energy says a large percentage of the electricity used to power electronics in the average American home is wasted on rechargers and plugged-in appliances that are not being used? TVs, computers, stereos, VCRs, toasters, and microwaves may look like they're innocently sitting there, but if they're plugged in, they're sucking watts. So unplug those rechargers. Use power strips on electronics. Or just pull the plug.

# Fourteen

## July 21

I was having my lunch break with Marissa today when Caitlin called to tell me there would be an emergency meeting tonight for the fund-raiser.

"But I'm working tonight," I told her.

"I thought you might be. But I wanted to call just in case."

"So what's the emergency?"

"Redemption is booked for another concert the same night."

"The same night?" I sneaked in a bite of my salad as I listened.

"Yes. Chloe wasn't too happy about it either. But apparently someone messed up, and according to their contract, there's no getting out of it."

"Can you get someone else?"

"The church worship band has offered to play." I could hear the disappointment in Caitlin's voice. "They're a great worship band and all but not really concert worthy."

"Wait a minute..." I set down my fork as realization hit.

"What?"

I glanced at Marissa, who was absently drinking her soda, but I could tell she was listening. "Hang on, Caitlin." I was tempted to take the phone over to a place where Marissa couldn't hear. But that might hurt her feelings. Plus I had planned to tell her, just not yet.

"Uh, Marissa, can you keep a secret?"

"A secret?" Her eyes lit up. "Of course!"

So I quickly explained about my dad coming to visit.

"Hey, that's cool. But I don't see why it's a big secret."

"Well, you know he's kind of a celebrity. In fact, I had planned to do a small dinner, and naturally you and your dad are invited."

I couldn't read her expression, but she nodded. "That's cool."

"So can you keep it under your hat for a while? I mean, even with your dad?"

"Sure."

I put the phone back up to my ear. "Here's the deal, Caitlin. My dad is going to be here when the fund-raiser is scheduled. And it's possible that I could ask him to—"

"A Nick Stark concert!" she shrieked.

"Can anyone hear you?"

She laughed. "Well, not unless the neighbors are eavesdropping. I'm alone at the moment."

"But the thing is...could we sort of keep it under wraps?"

"Under wraps?"

"You know, like could we call it a mystery concert and not say who is playing? Or if the posters are already printed, could we go ahead and let people think that Redemption is playing but then spring my dad at the last minute with an explanation?"

"Why do you want to keep it so top secret, Maya?"

"Well...I guess I sort of wanted his visit to be low-key. You know, it's been kind of nice just being an average, normal girl."

Caitlin laughed. "I hate to inform you of this, Maya, but you are not just an average, normal girl. Whether your dad's a celebrity or not, you're the kind of person that people notice. Plus you've got your newspaper column, which was quite good this weekend."

"Thanks." I stabbed my fork into a cucumber and bit into it.

"Besides, I think it would be unfair to the ticket buyers. Redemption is a Christian rock band that appeals to young people, and that's cool. But Nick Stark could appeal to lots of older people, ones who wouldn't even think to come to hear Redemption. In fact, this could be huge. With Nick Stark here, the stadium would probably sell out."

"Maybe..."

"But if it's a problem for you, I understand."

Suddenly I envisioned a crowd of impoverished school kids with no new backpacks or school supplies, and I felt very, very selfish.

"No, I'm okay with it. But before you do anything, I'd better check with my dad."

"Oh, I can just see God's hand in this, Maya."

"Yeah, maybe." So I told her good-bye and looked back at Marissa.

She grinned. "So you were going to keep your big-time celebrity daddy all to yourself, were you?"

"No, it's not like that. I mean, he's coming here for a break, and he's had a pretty full—"

"I heard you, Maya. You just want to be an average, normal girl." I could hear the teasing note in her voice now.

"Thanks a lot." I turned my attention back to my lunch now.

"Sorry. I couldn't resist. But it is pretty funny. I mean, you will never be an average, normal girl. You're way too good-looking. You've got too much money. And just this afternoon as we were walking through the mall, I saw at least a dozen guys checking you out."

"They were probably looking at you."

She laughed. "Hey, I know I get my fair share of looks, Maya, but those long legs of yours and that mane of hair... Well, most of the looks were aimed at you."

"Yeah...whatever."

"So why not just go with the flow?"

"The flow?"

"Yeah. Your dad's famous. Big deal. Get over yourself."

Okay, that made me laugh. "Thanks. I needed that."

"That's what friends are for."

"I wish you hadn't graduated already," I said. The more I consider going to high school, the more I realize that I won't have any friends. Well, besides Dominic.

She rolled her eyes. "Not me. I'm so glad to be out of that prison."

"So have you decided about college?" Marissa's dad wants her to go to the university where she was accepted. But she's considering hanging out here and doing community college.

"I don't know. Sometimes I think, yeah, I'll just pack it up and go to the university. But then I'd be stuck in a dorm with some stupid roommate, and I'm not sure I could handle that. It might be easier just to stay here."

"That surprises me," I admitted.

"Why?"

"I think of you as the party girl, going away to school, living on campus... Well, it seems you'd like that."

"Do you want to know the truth, daddy's girl?"

I frowned. "Hey, I'm not exactly a daddy's girl."

"Maybe not...but the truth is, maybe I am."

I stopped drinking my green tea and looked up. "What?"

"Well, I'm worried about leaving him alone. I mean, I know I'm a pain, but my dad likes having me around. And I help out some too."

Okay, I couldn't imagine Marissa helping out, but why would she lie about it? Still, I was too surprised to say anything.

"Fine. Now you know my secret, and I know yours. I guess we're both daddy's girls." She kind of smiled. "I never admit it, but my old man's not so bad—even if he is a cop. And I know he loves me. He's just worried that I'm going to mess up so badly that I won't be able to get out of it. I keep telling him that as soon as he lightens up on me, I'll probably be more responsible."

"How's that?"

"It's like this. If you have a controlling parent who's always warning you not to blow it or telling you how to live your life, you don't need to think for yourself. They do it for you, right?"

I considered this. "In a way that makes sense. My mom was pretty checked out, and that forced me to be hyperresponsible."

"See!" She pointed her fork at me. "Just what I'm saying."

Marissa's theory might actually hold water. I mean, I suppose I am more mature as a result of Shannon's lack of parenting skills. Still, I don't exactly feel like writing her a thank-you letter just yet.

## July 22

Dad returned my call this morning. And when I asked him about the benefit concert, he actually sounded pleased. Well, pleased and tired.

"How are you holding up?"

"Okay, but I'm counting the days until next week. What night is the concert?"

"Saturday, August second."

"That's good. I'll have a few days to rest up."

"So you really want to do it?"

"I'm honored that you want me there, honey."

I told him about the backpack project, and he seemed even happier to help out. By the time we hung up, I realized that Caitlin was probably right—God's hand is in this. I called and told her the good news, and she was ecstatic.

"That's so great. And fortunately, the posters hadn't been

printed yet. It was a scheduling error at the print shop, but I think God was trying to save everyone a few bucks. I'll call them right now, and hopefully we can start putting up posters by the end of the week. It's pretty short notice—only eleven days away."

"Hey, Dominic wants to be on the committee," I told her.

"Great, we need more hands."

"I'll bring him to the meeting on Thursday."

"Awesome. Uh, Maya?"

"What?"

"I hate to be a nag, but did you read those verses about forgiveness?"

I looked at my open Bible. "Yes..."

"And?"

"And...I'm working on it. But I do have a question."

"What?"

"What if you feel like you can't forgive someone?"

"Then you ask God to help you."

"Okay, well...what about asking for forgiveness? Isn't Brooke supposed to apologize and ask me to forgive her?"

There was a long pause now.

"I mean, that's what we do with God, right?"

"Yes, although God was always offering that forgiveness to us—just ready and waiting for us to wake up and come get it."

"I suppose..."

"Josh asked Brooke if she planned to ask you for forgiveness, Maya."

"What did she say?"

"To be honest, she seemed kind of mad at you."

"Mad at me?"

"Yes. She said you had said mean things to her."

"I said mean things to her?"

"That's what she said."

"Well."

"Anyway, you can't control what Brooke does or says or thinks, Maya. You can only control yourself. And if you refuse to forgive her, it only hurts you."

"The wall thing?"

"Yes. Your unforgiveness will come between you and God. This is a fact of life. Not only that, but you'll suffer in other ways too. Refusing to forgive someone robs us of joy—and peace."

Okay, I knew she was right about that. For weeks I've felt like I have this black Brooke cloud hanging over me. Even with the lawsuit put aside, the cloud remains. In fact, it seems to be getting bigger.

"Here's what I'll do," I said slowly. "I will really pray about it. And this time I'll ask God to help me."

"That's good, Maya. Really, it's the best you can do."

I know God is God and very powerful, but it'll take a miracle to make me forgive Brooke. And to know that she's going around telling others that I've been mean to her—well, that just fries me!

## July 24

Dominic and I went to the planning meeting together. It was fun having him there, seeing him make suggestions and offer to help. I could tell Caitlin appreciated it too. Then afterward in the church parking lot, Dominic walked me around to the passenger's side and was about to open the door (he's polite like that), and suddenly we were embracing and kissing. With my back to the car, I could feel the whole pressure of his body against mine, and it literally took my breath away—in a tingly, electrical way. Finally I gently but firmly pushed him away.

"Sorry," he said in a husky voice. "I didn't mean to do that."

"I know." I waited for him to open the door, then got in. I didn't know what to say, so I just sat there as he drove me home.

He walked me to the front door. "Are we still on for tomorrow night?"

"Sure," I said quickly. Mostly I wanted to get inside the house before we were suddenly kissing again. "See you at eight?"

"I'll be there." He leaned forward and gave me a quick peck on the cheek. "How's that?"

I smiled at him. "Perfect."

Maybe things weren't as carried away as they seemed. Still, I can't believe Dominic and I had a big make-out session in the church parking lot of all places! Fortunately I don't think anyone saw us. Even so, it's a little unsettling. What if we had been someplace private? Someplace where no one could see us? What if things just kept going, getting hotter and hotter? That's enough to make me quit writing tonight. I'll have to think about that tomorrow. It seems I put off a lot of things to think about until the next day. Even my promise to ask God to help me forgive Brooke has been delayed time after time. I'm beginning to wonder if I'm much of a Christian. Maybe I'm just faking it. I remember how aggravated I was at Brooke and Amanda when we worked on the mural. Like I kept thinking they were both fake Christians. Now I wonder if I'm not a lot more like them than I care to admit.

## Maya's Green Tip for the Day

Speaking of faking it. Can your rear end tell the difference between toilet paper that's made from recycled paper or TP that's made from "virgin" paper? Mine sure can't. But that may be because I've been using the recycled stuff for years. According to the National Resources Defense Council (NRDC), if every American household replaced just one roll (500 sheets) of virgin-fiber toilet paper with 100 percent recycled paper (just one roll!), we'd save almost half a million trees! I say it's worth a try. And who knows, one roll might lead to another…and another.

# Fifteen

"Get a load of this." Caitlin held up a bright orange poster announcing Nick Stark was performing at the benefit concert next weekend. It was a little past three when she'd shown up unexpectedly at Jacqueline's.

"Very cool," I said as I studied the screen-printed poster. The image of my dad was an interesting style, but it was definitely him with his wire-rimmed shades and close-cropped hair.

"Can you put up a poster here in the shop?"

"Of course," said Jackie as she emerged from behind the counter. "We can put up a couple if you like. One on that window, and another over there might be nice."

"Great."

I introduced Jackie to Caitlin, and they both went on and on about how great it was that Nick Stark was coming to town. Okay, I tried not to look too distressed over this. Because really, I'm fine with it. Still, it makes me nervous when people start to gush.

"When's your lunch break?" Caitlin asked me.

"You can take it now, if you like," said Jackie. "Business is pretty slow at the moment."

"Are you sure?" I said.

She smiled. "Positive. Go and enjoy."

So I went with Caitlin to get some lunch. Fortunately, Marissa wasn't coming by today. And I wouldn't see Dominic until after work. We got our food and found a table in a quiet corner of the food court, and as we started to eat, Caitlin brought up Dominic. "I just dropped a bunch of posters at his house. He's going to spend the next few hours putting them up."

"Cool."

"Then he said he's got a big date with you."

My cheeks grew warm. "He's meeting me here after work. At eight. We're going to catch a flick, I think."

"So...how's it going with him?"

"Okay..."

Caitlin smiled. "I think I'll just cut to the chase."

"The chase?"

"Yeah, I couldn't help but notice you two last night."

"Last night?" I could hear the pitch of my voice get a little higher.

"Yeah. Josh actually saw you guys first. He said it looked like Dominic was having way too much fun."

"He said that?"

"Well, just to me. No one else was around."

"Oh..."

"But I was concerned, Maya. Are you okay with this?"

"With what?" I looked down and forked my cheese ravioli like I was starving.

"With how intimate you and Dominic seem to be getting."

Okay, I could have lied to her. But I really didn't want to.

"It's kind of bothering me."

She nodded as she opened her dressing packet and squirted it over her salad. "That's what I suspected."

"I just don't know what to do about it. I mean, I was about to say something last night right after it happened. But we just drove home in silence, which is another thing that bugs me. But then he was a perfect gentleman when he walked me to the door. He gave me a little kiss on the cheek and said good night."

"That's sweet."

"Still, I can't pretend that I'm not part of the problem. I mean, I'm sure I enjoy kissing as much as he does."

She kind of giggled. "That's pretty normal."

"But I am getting worried that it could go too far. I know what you said about Beanie and everything."

"Can I tell you another story?"

"Sure." I nodded in relief. "Go for it."

So she told me about how she and Josh started dating during high school. "Ironically, I kind of stole him from a good friend." She shook her head. "Not that I exactly knew this at the time. But I did later."

"You stole Josh from a friend?" Somehow this did not sound like the Caitlin I knew.

"Yes. It's kind of embarrassing to admit it now, but back then my friend Jenny and I were competing for the same guy. But Josh liked me better."

"Apparently."

She laughed. "And I obviously liked him a lot too. In fact, I knew that I was in love—and that was pretty scary."

"Why?"

"Because we were so young. Oh sure, we thought we were old at the time. I was seventeen. He was a senior. Even so, I knew we were too young to be that serious. Plus I had made an abstinence pledge to God, and I was determined to keep it. But dating Josh put my pledge in serious jeopardy."

"Meaning you and Josh thought about having sex?"

"What I didn't know back then was that Josh had already had sex...with his previous girlfriend, Jenny. Later on, Josh told me that had set him up to expect to have sex again. With me."

"So what did you do?"

"Well, after some pretty steamy dates, I knew that God was telling me it was time to break up."

"You broke up with Josh?"

Caitlin slowly nodded. "Yes. And trust me, it wasn't easy."

"Was Josh hurt?"

"Well, I tried to explain my reasoning to him. I told him that

I took my abstinence pledge seriously and that dating him was not helping. And although Josh wasn't happy about the breakup, he told me years later how much he respected me for doing it."

"And obviously, you didn't break up permanently."

"Obviously." She smiled. "But after I broke up with Josh, I realized that I didn't want to continue dating anyone."

"Because you loved Josh?"

"Because I loved God."

I watched her, and I knew she was telling me more than just words. She was talking about her heart and her convictions, and these are things she takes very seriously.

"I knew that to continue dating would probably put my relationship with God at risk, as well as my vow to save sex for marriage. I'd seen up close and personal how difficult it was to maintain a healthy relationship with Josh. And he'd be the first one to tell you—or anyone—that his hormones were like a wildfire, and he'd also tell you that I did him a huge favor when I broke up with him."

"But you did get back together?"

"Not until my senior year in college. By then we'd both grown up a lot. Josh had started taking his relationship with God seriously. He'd gone to Bible school. And when we finally got back together, well, I can't even tell you how thankful I was that we'd done this right." She sighed. "I'm not saying that we didn't have problems or that everything was easy. But doing it God's way has made a huge difference in our marriage."

I sighed. "Well, I have to admit that when I see you guys together, it seems like you have a really great relationship. Probably the most solid marriage I've ever seen."

"Thanks to God's help."

There was a long pause now. We both just quietly ate our food, but I had a lot to think about.

"So what do you think I should do?" I finally asked her.

"I can't tell you what to do, Maya. All I can tell you is what worked for me. And what's happened to others I know. I'm sure you've heard about my brother Ben...and Natalie."

I pressed my lips together and nodded. I knew that Natalie and Ben had dated and that Natalie had gotten pregnant, but I'd been shocked to hear that they had actually gotten married. Although Nat never spoke of it. Kim only told me because she thought it might help me understand Nat better. And I must admit that I felt sorry for Nat when Kim told me how the marriage was such a mess and that Ben had started drinking and was abusive. Eventually they split up, and Natalie gave the baby up for adoption. And sometimes, when Nat isn't lecturing me about being a Christian, I see the sadness in her eyes and wonder how it would feel to have been through all that as a teenager. It pretty much blows my mind.

"How is Ben doing?" I said.

"He's still struggling. But he rededicated his life to God, and I think, in time, he'll be okay. I think he learned a lot."

"That's a hard way to learn."

"Just my point. Life throws plenty of hard things at us, Maya. You know for yourself that's true. So I don't see any reason to go around inviting them in. I have never regretted keeping my vow to wait until marriage to have sex."

"But wasn't it hard to give up dating?"

"Sometimes. But I still did fun things with guys. And in a way, it allowed me to get to know my Christian guy friends better because they knew what the rules were. It eliminated some pressure."

I glanced at my watch and realized my lunch break was almost over. So I thanked Caitlin for telling me this.

"Oh, I almost forgot," she said as we both got up. "I can't do our Saturday session tomorrow. Josh and I are driving over to Brenton for a wedding."

"I think we just had our Saturday session." I frowned. "And now I'm getting worried about my date with Dominic tonight. I'm not sure how it will go."

"Why don't you just talk to him, Maya? Tell him how you feel and what worries you. See how he reacts."

I nodded and picked up my bag.

"I'll be praying for you."

Now I'll cut to the chase. I had planned to do what Caitlin said, to talk to him. But suddenly we were sitting in the back row of the theater. Dominic's arm was around me, and then we were kissing. I missed most of the movie. Afterward, I told him that I needed to get home.

"I've got a lot to do tomorrow," I told him as he drove me back to my car, "to get things ready for my dad's visit."

So now I'm sitting here writing this, and I feel like I totally blew it. But maybe I can figure it out tomorrow.

## July 28

I think I've been allowing my busyness to distract me from dealing with a couple of problems. I will write down my problems, just to keep me from forgetting them altogether. Not that it's likely to happen.

1. I need to figure out how to forgive Brooke Marshall.
2. I need to be honest with Dominic about my concerns.

But at least I've been praying about both situations. And eventually I'll know what to do about them, but I'm in no hurry. In the meantime I'm working either at the boutique or in the garden, which I want to get perfect. Or else I'm helping with the fund-raiser or organizing my dinner party where I'll introduce Dad to my friends. And then I have to get my column turned in to Uncle Allen on Wednesdays. So life is pretty busy. Or else I'm just using all this as an excuse. Time will tell.

Another distraction popped into my life today. Caitlin called me and asked if I could do something to promote the benefit concert.

"Sure, what?" I asked.

"Well, it would be on your day off. Thursday, right?"

"Right."

"A friend of mine at Channel Five wants to do a quick spot about the concert, and I thought it would be cool to have Nick Stark's daughter do the promotion."

"Me? On TV?" Okay, I was not liking this.

"Yes. Would you mind?"

"I'm not sure this is—"

"Look, I knew you'd be reluctant, Maya, and that you might give me that bit about wanting to be an average, normal girl. But just think of those kids you'd be doing this for. So far our ticket sales haven't been too great. I know it's because we got the posters out late. My news friend, Suzy, says that having you on the news could reach a lot of viewers, and the concert might actually sell out."

"So you're basically guilting me into this?"

"No, but I would encourage you to pray about it. And if you could decide by morning, it would be helpful. If you don't do it, I'll go in. Of course, I'll have to cancel a counseling appointment to do that and—"

"Fine, fine," I said quickly. "I'll do it." And really, I told myself after I hung up, it couldn't be any worse than modeling. Then I remembered Marissa's advice: "Get over yourself, Maya." And so I will.

## July 31

I did the news spot this morning, and it was actually kind of fun. To my surprise it was much easier than modeling.

"You're really good at this," Suzy told me after we wrapped it up.

The camera guy nodded. "She's a natural."

"Thanks," I told them. "I just hope that it sells some tickets."

"I'm buying two," the camera guy said.

"So am I," Suzy said.

I laughed. "Four tickets—we're on our way."

"We'll run this spot on the news tonight," Suzy promised. "And I'll talk to the station manager about running it as a public service announcement for the next couple of days."

"Great," I said, thanking them again.

"Thank you!" Suzy said. "You made my job easy."

And so, when it was all said and done, I felt pretty good about how it all went this morning. But I didn't feel so good when I left the studio. I realized that it was located on the other side of the hill where Brooke lives. I remembered how I'd driven over to her house on another day off, a day not so different from today. I was so enraged when I saw her. Naturally, it seemed justified to me. But it might've felt different to her. And to be honest, I can't remember exactly what I said to her. I know I shouted. But so did she. Still, Caitlin's right. I need to do whatever it takes to forgive her. So I actually started to drive up her street, but then I lost my nerve, turned my car around on a cul-de-sac, and headed home.

I just could not make myself do it. Maybe I need to pray some more. Also, and this is the truth, I'm still a little ticked that she hasn't apologized to me. Didn't her dad promise Mr. Bernard

that she would? Of course, maybe Brooke, like me, is simply waiting for the right moment...or maybe she's waiting until an apology might actually be sincere. Who knows?

Besides, my dad arrives tonight, and I still have a few details
to take care of for the dinner party tomorrow. So really, I don't
have time to deal with Brooke right now. Dominic is coming to
the dinner tomorrow, and we haven't seen much of each other
this past week—we've both been too busy. Maybe I don't really
need to be worried about our relationship at all.

## Maya's Green Tip for the Day

Okay, I'll admit it was really hot today. And while I appreciate the fact that my home and place of work have air
conditioning, I do not get why some people keep the
temperature so cold. For every degree you turn up your
AC, you save 3 percent on your electric bill. That could
add up to millions of dollars and kilowatts across the
country. So why freeze when you can save money and
energy by turning it up?

# Sixteen

## August 1

I picked up my dad at the airport last night at seven. I offered to take him on a tour of the town, but he declined.

"I think I'd like to call it a night, if you don't mind, Maya."

"No problem. You look pretty exhausted."

"I've been up for about twenty hours now."

So I drove him downtown where he'd reserved a room at, according to Uncle Allen, the best hotel around. But probably not nearly as nice as the places my dad usually stays. "It's not the Ritz," I told him as I pulled up in front, "but hopefully you'll be comfortable."

"I'll be asleep before my head hits the pillow." He pulled his bag from the trunk. "And I'll probably sleep in tomorrow too. I hope you don't mind."

"You just call me when you want to, Dad." Then we hugged, and he went into the hotel. I have the next five days off, but it's not like I planned to spend every free minute with him. He needs to rest up a little before the concert tomorrow. But at least he seemed excited about my dinner party.

I've been working all day to make everything perfect. It's been kind of a relief that Dad slept in until nearly two. Then he called to say that he'd decided to take it easy until dinnertime. The plan is for Dominic to pick him up and bring him over here around six. Uncle Allen offered but then remembered he needed to be here to tend the barbecue.

I put the finishing touches outside. I rented four tables and sixteen chairs and arranged them around the backyard. Because Aunt Patricia liked to sew, she had a whole trunk full of fabrics, and Kim helped me pick out the prints that looked most Hawaiian for the tablecloths. I'm going with a luau theme. I picked flowers from the garden to make colorful bouquets for the tables. For vases, I used recycled tin cans wrapped with big elephant ear bamboo leaves and tied with raffia. Jackie loaned me tiki torches that I planted randomly around the yard. I also made hanging votive candleholders from recycled glass jars and wire and beads. It's going to look magical once it starts to get dark. And for music, Uncle Allen dug out some Hawaiian CDs that they got on vacation a few years ago.

"Everything looks beautiful," Kim said.

"Thanks." I looked around the backyard with satisfaction. This yard isn't nearly as big or fancy as where I lived in Beverly Hills (well, back in the days when we could afford a groundskeeper), but I still like it better here. It feels homey and sweet...and safe.

"The caterer just delivered the food," Kim said. "I stashed it in the fridge. It looks really good."

"I want this to be special." I adjusted one of the flower arrangements. "You know, for my dad."

"I can't wait to meet him, Maya." She clapped her hands like a little girl. "This is so exciting!"

I glanced over to the fence that separates our yard from Natalie's. "Did you invite her?" Nat wanted to come, and although I wasn't that thrilled with the idea, out of respect for Kim I had said it was okay.

"Actually, she invited herself." Kim shook her head. "And her mom too. Her mom is a Nick Stark fan. I told Nat I'd have to check with you."

I forced a smile. "Great, that means all the tables will be filled."

"You're sure?"

I nodded. "Absolutely."

Kim looked hugely relieved. "Thanks. I better tell her so they can arrange for a sitter."

I almost said, "Oh, the kids can come too," except I know how wild and crazy Nat's younger siblings can be. I like them. But I want tonight to be more grown-up.

"Are you going to have assigned seating?" Kim asked as we went inside.

"Yes. The place cards are in my room."

"Let me guess, recycled paper?"

I laughed. "Yes. And I'm going to glue little flowers on them."

"How did you get to be so clever, Maya?"

"Probably from being homeschooled the past few years."

"But I thought you said that Shannon was, well, you know, kind of checked out?"

"She was. I pretty much homeschooled myself. And I probably spent more time on art than math."

"And yet you aced your PSATs." Now she looked curiously at me. "So have you decided whether you're going to high school or college next year?"

Besides the guidance counselor at Harrison High, Kim and Uncle Allen are the only ones I've discussed this with. And lately I haven't said much. Everyone else, including Dominic, assumes I'll be in high school next year. They don't know I already have my GED and passed my PSAT.

"I don't know," I said. "Sometimes I think I should keep working part-time for Jackie and start taking community college classes and make plans for getting an apartment and being on my own."

Kim nodded without commenting.

"And other times I just want to have a normal high-school experience. You know, kind of like you."

She smiled. "You only get one chance to do that, Maya. I mean, college and career are always out there, but you can only do high school when you're a teenager."

Now I'm thinking about that as I'm chilling in my room. It's still a couple of hours before my little soiree, and everything is ready—I've even finished the place cards for the tables. And I'm hoping everything will turn out okay. But I'm also thinking about what Kim said—that you can only do high school when you're a teenager. After that you can go to college for as long as you like. And you can work as long as you like. But high school is a one-time thing.

## August 2

Last night was wonderful. If I do say so myself, I think I might have a flair for entertaining. Not onstage kind of entertaining. I'll leave that to my dad. But everyone who came to the dinner party couldn't believe that I—a teenage girl—actually put the whole thing together. Like, afterward, Nat's mom was thanking my uncle. "You put together such a wonderful evening, Allen."

"This is all Maya's doing," he said with what seemed like an almost paternal sort of pride. She looked surprised. But then I pointed out that Uncle Allen had been responsible for the barbecue and Kim had helped in all sorts of ways.

But back to the beginning. Dominic brought my dad about thirty minutes before the other guests were supposed to arrive. I could tell that the two of them had already hit it off. Of course, this shouldn't surprise me since Dominic is a musician as well. I wonder why I hadn't thought of that before. But my dad really liked my uncle and cousin too. And they seemed to like him a lot. It felt like we really were family. I can't even describe how cool that was. I almost regretted that I'd invited others to join us since we were already having a great time with just our small group. But to my relief, it only got better as more guests arrived. It was so awesome to let Dad get a sample of my life and meet my friends. And once my friends got over being slightly star-struck, it was pretty fun. It got even better as the sky grew dark and all the tiki torches and candles were glowing, with Hawaiian music playing in the background.

"It's like a tropical fairyland out here," Kim said as the caterers began serving dessert—a combination of pineapple, coconut, and ice cream and very yummy. Kim and Uncle Allen and Dad and I were seated at the same table. I felt a tiny bit selfish for doing this—but, hey, he's my dad.

I put Dominic and Eddie with Marissa and her dad, and really, that seemed to go well. I could tell Marissa's dad was enjoying himself. I think he appreciated spending time with his daughter in a fairly happy setting. I put the Bernards at a table with Josh and Caitlin. And Nat and her mother sat with Pastor Tony and his wife, Stephanie.

To say that a good time was had by all wouldn't be an exaggeration. Okay, it got a little dicey when Nat's mom kept urging my dad to sing for us. I finally had to step in.

"Anyone who wants to hear Nick Stark sing will need to buy tickets for tomorrow's benefit concert," I announced loudly.

"That's right," Kim agreed.

"Good luck," Caitlin called from her table. "I heard that we're sold out."

This was followed by a loud cheer.

So even though I was pretty worn-out after the party ended, I was very happy. I think it went as well as possible. Dominic offered to drive my dad back to his hotel, but I told him that I wanted to.

"Why don't you just come along with us?" Dominic suggested.

"Thanks, but I'd like a little time with my dad alone." And okay, I could tell that Dominic was slightly hurt by this. But like I said, he's my dad. And I think I deserve some one-on-one.

"What a great evening." Dad leaned back in the passenger seat beside me.

"I hope we didn't wear you out."

"Not at all. In a way it was very refreshing."

"Refreshing?"

He nodded. "Yes. You have no idea how much it puts this father's heart at ease to see you with these people, Maya." His voice choked slightly now. "Allen and Kim are really great—and the rest of your friends." He sniffed. "Well, I just couldn't be more pleased and relieved."

"They're a nice bunch of people."

"I know this will sound trite, Maya, but tonight has helped restore my faith in the human race."

"It doesn't sound trite, Dad. I know what you mean."

"I can't imagine you landing in a better place, honey."

"Me either."

"Allen told me that you're welcome to stay as long as you need to."

"Even after Kim goes to college?"

"I asked the same thing, Maya."

"And?"

"Allen paid you a very high compliment."

"So are you going to tell me?"

"He said that if it was anyone besides you, he wouldn't even consider taking a teenager into his home. But he said you remind him of Kim. He said that you're mature beyond your years, and with your independence he wouldn't feel he needed to take care of you."

"That was nice."

"But he was concerned."

"About what?"

"Well, he wondered if you'd be very happy living there. He thought you deserved to live with a more normal family."

"A more normal family?" I had to laugh. "Uncle Allen and Kim are the most normal people I know."

"Yes, but Kim will be gone. And you might not be comfortable living with your widowed uncle." He glanced at me.

"Uncle Allen is the sweetest man I know." I looked at Dad. "Present company excluded. I feel perfectly safe and comfortable with him, if that's what you mean."

"It's just that you've been through so much, Maya. I know you haven't given up on your emancipation plan. And I think you're proving that you're able to take care of yourself."

"I've been taking care of myself for years."

He sighed. "I know...and I'm sorry."

"No, I wasn't trying to make you feel bad."

"But my concert schedule doesn't seem to be lightening up any. And there's no telling what will happen with your mother's appeal this fall."

"Meaning?"

"Meaning...maybe you would be safest if you were emancipated. That way you could continue living with your uncle or be on your own, but Shannon couldn't exercise any parental rights over you."

"Yes, I've thought the same thing."

"I'll do or sign anything to help you get this, Maya."

"Thanks, Dad."

We were at his hotel by then. I got out and hugged him.

"Thanks for one of the best nights of my life." He still had tears in his eyes. "You made me so proud tonight." He used his handkerchief to dab his nose. "I know you're going to be okay."

I nodded. "Do you want to just take it easy tomorrow? You know, because of the concert?"

"I'll sleep in. My crew is supposed to get here around noon. Then we'll have to set up in the stadium and do some sound checks and all that. But maybe you and I could have an early dinner together."

"Sure. Just let me know when and where."

He hugged me again, kissing me on the cheek. "You're a great kid, Maya. You make me proud to be your dad."

And this afternoon as I write this, I'm thinking it's cool that Dad is so proud of me. I want to feel as confident as he does, but I'm not always so sure. I mean, I'm only sixteen and a half. Who knows what could still go wrong? I try not to think about things with Dominic. Or my dilemma with Brooke. It feels like a lot of pressure. And something else is bothering me quite a bit—the wall that Caitlin warned me about. I am convinced that I have been steadily building that wall by not forgiving Brooke. And now I'm not even sure how to put an end to it. But I'm praying, and I hope God will show me. I doubt I'll be able to deal with it until after my dad's visit. Still, it must be resolved because I NEED God. I really, really need God. I can't afford not to have Him in my life. I can't bear to do it on my own. I've been there and done that. And it didn't work.

## August 3

Last night's fund-raiser was a screaming success. I didn't expect there would be so many Nick Stark fans in this town. Apparently I was wrong. And okay, most of the concert attendees were older folks, like forty and up. But according to my dad, that's usually the case. Still, it was pretty cool. When Dad called me onto the stage to join him, I couldn't help but feel proud of him—and proud of my connection with him. Really, it was awesome. And, oh yeah, we made a boatload of money. So not only will we be getting backpacks and school supplies for kids in need but coats and shoes as well. How cool is that?

This morning Dad went to church with me. And to my surprise, Mr. and Mrs. Marshall came up to meet him. Brooke wasn't with them, but still I was speechless. Fortunately, Mr. Marshall initiated the introductions. Then I managed to mutter, "These are Brooke's parents."

Dad nodded solemnly.

"We wanted to apologize to you personally," Mr. Marshall said to my dad. "We are terribly sorry for the ordeal that our daughter has put both you and Maya through."

"Thank you." My dad nodded politely. But there was a coolness to it.

"And we saw your concert last night," gushed Mrs. Marshall. "Just wonderful."

"Thank you again."

Then Caitlin brought her in-laws over, and fortunately, we were distracted by introductions to the Millers.

"My mother-in-law is a huge fan," said Caitlin, "and she was dying to meet you."

"We're both fans," said Mr. Miller, "and last night was fantastic."

"Their daughter's band was supposed to play," I explained, filling him in about the double-booking.

"And don't tell Chloe," said Mrs. Miller, "but their loss was our gain."

Finally I managed to extract my dad from the throng of fans. Some old and, after last night, some new. We went and got some lunch, and then I took him on a driving tour of the town.

"It's charming," he said when we finally ended up at home, where we planned to spend a laid-back afternoon. "It reminds me of an old fifties sitcom, like *Leave It to Beaver*."

"Is that good or bad?"

"I think it's fantastic."

I smiled. "So do I."

The weather (high seventies with a nice breeze) was perfect for hanging in the backyard. I showed my dad some of the things I was working on in the garden, then we had iced tea, and before long my dad was snoozing in the chaise lounge—totally relaxed.

I slipped back into the house where Uncle Allen and Kim were puttering in the kitchen. "What's up?" I asked.

"We want to fix you guys dinner tonight," Kim said.

"Is that okay?" my uncle asked. "We thought it would be more relaxing for Nick not to be mobbed by fans."

And he was right. It was very relaxing. He grilled kabobs, some with meat and some without. We lit the torches and candles once again, and it was perfectly delightful.

## Maya's Green Tip for the Day

Here's how you can make your own hanging glass-jar votive candleholders. Find some glass jars in a variety of sizes (like from mayo or jam or mustard or spaghetti sauce). Peel off the labels and wash the jars (or add them to a load that's going through the dishwasher, since that conserves water). Then take some wire—it can be any-thing, though recycled is best of course. But if you want to be fancy, you can use copper. Get a few clear glass beads for fun. Now wrap the wire around the jar's mouth, use a pencil to make wire curlicues for decoration, add some beads here and there, and attach a wire handle (if you want it to hang like a lantern). Then place a votive candle in the bottom of each jar. Set them on tables or hang them from trees. When the sun goes down, light the candles, and you have a fairyland backyard.

# Seventeen

## August 5

I took my dad back to the airport this morning, and although I was sad to see him go, I felt slightly relieved to get back to my "normal" life. I mean, it was more fun than I expected to have my celebrity dad in town. But I was ready for life to settle back into my comfortable routines, and I was happy to go back to work.

"Welcome back," Jackie said cheerfully. "You've been missed."

"You have no idea," said her daughter, Rosemary.

"I'm sorry," I said. "Did you have to work a lot of extra hours?"

Rosemary laughed. "No, not missed like that."

"You've been missed by customers," Jackie said. "It seems you have your own fan base."

"My own fan base?"

"Yes. So many people saw you on that TV spot and then again at the concert."

"And then there's your green column in the paper," Rosemary added, "which I must say is really good.".

"So it seems you're the new celebrity around here."

I frowned.

"Don't you want to be a celebrity?" asked Rosemary.

"Not really... I just want everything to go back to normal."

They both laughed.

And as the day progressed, it seemed more and more that normal was slipping between my fingers. Not only were customers treating me differently, but when I checked my phone messages on my lunch break, several were from Suzy Richards at Channel Five News. I figured it was related to the concert and maybe they wanted to do some kind of follow-up, but when I called her, she was up to something completely different.

"I spoke to your uncle today, Maya, about your green column in the paper."

"You read that?"

"Sure. It's great."

"Oh." Still, I was confused.

"And I've been thinking there must be a better way for you to get more people concerned about conservation and recycling and all that stuff."

"How?"

"TV."

I wasn't sure how to respond.

"Yes, I know you're not that excited about being the center of attention, Maya. You made that clear when you came in here."

"That's right."

"But the problem was that you were so great at it." She chuckled.

"Yes, but—"

"So your uncle and I were talking, and we both felt that if you really care about recycling and this town, well, you should be willing to sacrifice."

"Sacrifice?"

"By doing a green spot on Channel Five News."

"A green spot?"

"Yes. Your uncle has agreed to share 'It's a Green Thing' with our TV station."

"He has?"

"Well, it was conditional. Naturally, we couldn't do it without you."

"I'm still not sure."

"Look, it's simple, Maya. You'd come in here and shoot, say, three spots all at once. And we'd run them on, say, Monday, Wednesday, Friday. You know, like three times a week."

"Uh-huh?"

"It would probably take only a couple of hours, maybe less since you're such a natural in front of the camera."

"But I—"

"Okay, before you put up obstacles, I want to point out something."

"And that is?"

"Well, you really do care about the environment, right?"

"Of course."

"And as you noticed, our city does not have curbside recycling, right?"

"Yes."

"What better way to get it than to have all our viewers being informed by you? My guess is that it'll be up and running by fall."

"Really?"

"The media has a huge influence. I'm sure you know that."

"But I'm not—"

"Oh yes," she said quickly, "I should tell you that there's money involved. I know you're working at Jacqueline's, but when school starts, it might be difficult to get in as many hours." She laughed. "Although with Nick Stark for a dad, I wouldn't think you'd be too desperate for money."

"I like being independent," I shot back at her.

"Good girl. Kudos for you."

"So what kind of money are you talking about?" I asked with a little more interest. After all, I still have my emancipation plan, and the court expects me to prove that I am self-supporting.

"Well, we haven't crunched numbers yet, Maya. But I think it's safe to assure you that you'd make more working for us than at the dress shop. And you'd be spending a lot less time doing it."

I considered this. With my newspaper column, doing a Channel Five News spot, and maybe just a few hours a week at Jacqueline's, I might be able to convince a judge that I was ready to support myself.

"So will you at least think about it, Maya?"

"Sure. Can I get back to you tomorrow?"

"Sounds great. And something else you might be interested in..."

"What's that?"

"We could set this up with your high school or even the community college as an internship so you'd get credits for it."

"Really?"

"Sure, we do it all the time."

"Okay. This is sounding better and better."

"Terrific. We'd really love to have you on our team, Maya. After you left last week, several people commented on what a natural you were and how easy you were to work with."

"Well, thanks..."

There's no denying that this was flattering. As I'm writing this, it occurs to me that just one year ago my life was totally miserable. I felt hopeless and scared, and the future seemed bleak. And yet here I am now. I can't help but think God is the one responsible. Which reminds me...I have unfinished business to take care of with Brooke. But I'm just not sure how to go about it. Do I go to her privately? Or would it be better to have her parents there? I don't feel like I can trust Brooke on her own. And her parents went out of their way to apologize to my dad. Unless that was simply their excuse for meeting him. But anyway, I think I'll try to arrange something. Maybe on my day off. On Thursday.

## August 7

But on Thursday, today, I found myself at Channel Five News again. This time I was taping my "It's a Green Thing" spot. As soon as I agreed to do this (yesterday), Suzy put together a contract and arranged the first taping. They will be scheduled on my days off until fall.

The taping ended up taking longer than we expected, almost four hours. We were all just trying to figure it out, and everyone had a different opinion. Suzy assured me that once we get this down, it won't be such an ordeal.

"And maybe we can film her at home," suggested Ron, the camera guy. "You know, doing some of the things she talks about."

"That's a great idea," agreed Suzy. So next week we'll be "on location" at the Peterson residence.

"But let me check with my uncle first," I said.

"I can do that for you," Suzy said, nodding to her assistant. "We'll need him to sign a waiver anyway."

It was nearly three when I finished, and I went out to the parking lot and looked up at the hill. I've tried to call the Marshalls' home several times, but I always get their machine. I keep imagining Brooke up there looking at her caller ID and deciding not to answer since she probably doesn't want to talk to me. So I decided just to drive on up and see if I could catch her at home. Maybe doing gymnastic flips into her pool. But when I got there, a young woman answered the door.

"Is Brooke here?" I asked, suddenly nervous.

"No." The girl studied me, then her eyes lit up. "Hey, are you the green girl in the newspaper?"

I forced a smile. "Yes."

"Cool." She nodded. "Very cool."

"So do you know when she'll be back?"

"I'm the house sitter. The Marshalls are on vacation for, like, about ten more days, I think. Up in Canada visiting the grandparents."

"Oh."

"Sorry."

"No," I said, actually feeling relieved. "That's okay."

But my relief faded as I realized this meant ten more days of putting up bricks between God and me. Then I thought, *No way!* I needed to resolve this sooner. So I called Caitlin and poured out my story.

"Oh, poor Maya. I didn't realize you were still dealing with that."

"Well, we've missed a few Saturdays."

"You can forgive Brooke without being face to face."

"Really? For some reason I thought it had to be in person."

"No, not at all, although that's often best. But sometimes it's impossible, for instance if the person who offended you has passed on or lives in another country."

"Or is incarcerated."

"Yes."

"So what do I do?"

"You just come before God, and you honestly tell Him that you want to forgive her."

"That's all?"

"Well, it's different for everyone. But that's pretty much it. It's mostly just a change of heart, Maya. Like one day you're angry and bitter at someone, and then you hand it over to God, and you're not."

"Just like that?"

She laughed. "Yeah. Pretty much."

"Okay..." So I thanked her, then drove to a nearby park and walked over and sat on a bench beneath a big tree. I tried to imagine Brooke, and I told God that I've had some pretty bad feelings and thoughts toward her. I confessed that sometimes I've hated her. Finally I told Him that I was tired of being angry at her. I said that I wanted to let it go, and I asked Him to help me. And just like that, it's like this load was lifted. I mean, it was so easy I wasn't even sure if it was for real. But as quickly as the load lifted, that old deep sense of peace came back, so I was certain it was God. And then it's like I saw that whole wall come tumbling down. Nothing stood between God and me.

Sure, I realize as I write this tonight that I still need to figure out this thing with Dominic. But I am convinced that God will guide me through that too. And to be honest, with all that's been going on with my dad's visit and the concert and everything, we haven't had a chance to fall into the big make-out-session trap lately. Still, he has asked me out tomorrow night. And who knows where that might go.

## August 9

Dominic and I had a fight at youth group tonight. Well, not right in the middle of youth group—that would be embarrassing. But out in the parking lot. And I suppose the fight actually started last night. We went out on Friday. Instead of the usual movie, Dominic took me to jazz in the park again, which was a relief. It was after eight by the time we got there, but we listened awhile and danced, and then Dominic wanted to take a walk. I suppose that should've clued me. At first we just strolled along, enjoying the evening and the sounds of the music in the distance. Dominic was saying lots of sweet things like "I've never known a girl like you, Maya." The next thing I knew, we were embracing, sort of swaying to the music, and then we were kissing. And it kept getting more and more intense until I finally pulled away from him and yelled, "Stop it!"

Naturally, that hurt his feelings. We walked back to our cars without speaking. Fortunately, I had driven to the park after work to meet him. So, after a crisp "good night," I got in my car and drove home. And I was mad. Okay, I was mad and confused.

When I met with Caitlin this morning, I dumped the whole story on her. She gave me that look, like she wanted to say, "I told you so," but fortunately she didn't.

"I'm sorry" was all she said.

"So it seems you were right to warn me." I frowned down at my empty coffee cup. "But what do I do now?"

She kind of laughed. "I can't tell you what to do, Maya. You need to listen to God, to think for yourself. And yes, of course you should weigh the things I've told you. But I'm not your conscience."

"I know."

She reached for my notebook and wrote down some more Bible verses. "You can read these when you get home. And then pray about it. I'm sure God will lead you."

So to change the subject, I told her about forgiving Brooke. "I can't believe how great it felt to unload that. It was like I'd been wearing a lead overcoat, and I took it off and was able to run free."

She nodded. "Forgiveness is like that. Holding back on it really weighs you down."

"And comes between you and God." I thought about the situation with Dominic again. "Sort of like when things go too far with Dominic. It's like I feel this heaviness on me again."

"I know exactly what you mean. Kind of like you picked up a load that's much too heavy for you to carry."

"Exactly."

"And God knows that. I think that's why He wants us to wait until marriage for sex. He knows that it will weigh us down and distract us from Him—and those are only a couple of reasons."

I nodded. "When my dad was here, we had a pretty cool talk. He told me how proud he was of me."

"He should be."

"But then I realized how much I don't want to let him down."

"Or yourself."

"Right. And I don't want to let down my uncle or Kim either." I paused to really consider my words. "It's like having a family around makes you want to be more responsible—not just for yourself but for them as well."

"Most people don't get that until they're older than you," she said. "Kids are usually in college before they start to make choices out of concern for their loved ones."

"Well, I've been hurt enough by my mom's choices... I guess I don't want to be like her."

"I don't think you need to worry about it."

So when Dominic didn't call today, I decided to drive to youth group on my own. I would've given Kim a ride, but she had to attend a recital for some of her music students. As I drove to the church, I was miffed that Dominic had made no attempt to call. Because I really felt he owed me an apology. So I decided that if he was at youth group, I would give him the cold shoulder. Just a subtle hint. And when I saw him, that's exactly what I did.

Then as soon as youth group ended, I took off to my car. But he came chasing after me.

"What is wrong with you?" he demanded.

"Me?"

"Yes. Why are you being like this?"

"Like what?" Okay, I knew that sounded pretty stupid.

"Like you suddenly hate me."

I put my hands on my hips and just stared at him. "I can't believe you don't know the answer to that, Dominic."

"What?" But even as he said this, he glanced off to the side, like he was uncomfortable.

"The park. Last night. And other times. I just think it's wrong that we get so...well...so physical."

"Why?"

Okay, I have to admit that when he said this, he seemed sincere. Like I really was blindsiding him with this little news flash.

"Why?" I repeated, trying to get my footing. "You think it's okay to act like that? Aren't you a Christian, Dominic?"

He nodded. "Of course. You know I am. But do you think that Christians don't have those, well, you know...those kinds of feelings? You think that Christians aren't passionate?"

"That's not what I'm saying."

"What then?" Now his face softened, and he moved closer, and I could tell he was thinking about putting his arm around me. But I pushed him away.

"See!" I pointed at him. "All you want to do is make out and get carried away, and who knows where it will get us?"

Then he laughed. And that really ticked me off.

"You think it's funny?"

"Kind of. What are you afraid of, Maya? Do you think you won't be able to control yourself?"

I punched him in the chest. Okay, not hard. But I wanted to. And again he just laughed.

"I really don't think this is funny."

"But you do seem to be blowing it out of proportion." He lowered his voice. "I think we just need to talk about it, Maya, to work it out. I'm sure we can—"

"No! I don't think so."

"So what are you saying?"

"I'm saying we need to break up."

Now he looked truly crushed. "Break up?"

I nodded, feeling tears coming. Because the truth is, I really do like Dominic. He's the nicest guy I know. Well, except for this.

"Why?"

"Because it's wrong. I can feel it's wrong. And I talked to Caitlin this morning, and she—"

"You told Caitlin about us?"

"Yes. She's mentoring me. I tell her everything."

Now he looked miffed.

"And maybe you need to talk to Josh," I shot at him. "I mean, you sit up there with him every Saturday night, leading worship with him and even sharing Bible verses and acting like Mr. Perfect Christian, but—"

"I don't act like Mr. Perfect Christian!"

"Okay, maybe that was unfair. But you put out an image, Dominic. And I'm sure some of the youth group kids would be a little shocked to see how you are, well, when no one is looking."

"You know what I think, Maya?" He sounded mad now.

"What?"

"I think you've decided that you're too good for me."

"That is so not true."

"All your celebrity and publicity are going to your head, and you are—"

"You are so full of it, Dominic Walsh!" And then I got into my car and drove away. I wanted to put the pedal to the metal and step on it, but I had some self-control. Why give him the pleasure of seeing that he'd made me lose it? Why waste the gas?

# Maya's Green Tip for the Day

Here are ways to conserve fuel when driving. Keep your car tuned—a tune-up can add 1 mile per gallon. Keep tires properly inflated—low tires can waste 1 mile per gallon as well as wear down your tires. Slow down—driving 65 miles per hour instead of 55 can waste up to 2 miles per gallon, plus you might risk a ticket. Avoid fast takeoffs—a jackrabbit start uses twice as much gas as a gradual start. Pace your driving—keeping it smooth and even can save up to 2 miles per gallon. Don't overuse your AC—it can cost you up to 2 miles per gallon. But open windows are about the same because of air drag. Avoid engine idling—turn it off if you have to idle more than a couple of minutes. Plan your trips—combine errands and avoid rush-hour traffic. Finally, join a carpool. Or ride your bike.

# Eighteen

## August 15

It's been a week since the big fight. Dominic hasn't called, and I'm not calling him. And here's the thing: while I do miss him, I feel relieved not to have to deal with that right now. It was a lot of pressure. And my life has had too much pressure these past few years. I'm happy to take a break from it. But still, I do miss him.

"I just don't get it," Marissa told me yesterday. She'd popped in for lunch, and shortly after we sat down, I told her about my decision to break up. "I mean Dominic is one of the few great guys. Why are you blowing him off like this?"

Naturally, I wished I hadn't opened my mouth. "You're right," I said. "You *don't* get it."

"You mean it's a Christian thing?" she teased. "Or maybe it's a green thing... Did Dominic forget to recycle something important?"

I kind of laughed, then decided to change the subject. "So how goes the community service?"

She frowned. "Don't ask."

"Why?" I grinned at her. "I gave you the dirt on my life. You can at least do the same."

"Fine." She made a face. "I've been scrubbing public toilets all week. Are you happy now?"

Okay, I had to control myself not to laugh. Instead, I took a bite of my bean burrito and nodded as if I were extremely sympathetic.

"Have you ever seen how filthy a county-park bathroom can get by mid-August when the temperature's been in the nineties for a couple of weeks?" She made an even worse face.

I considered this. "I'm not sure, but I'd probably try to avoid them."

"Seriously disgusting. Disturbingly nasty. Frighteningly foul. Do you want to hear what I found in one of the stalls yesterday?"

"Thanks anyway, but I'm trying to eat here." I nodded to my lunch.

"Yeah, me too. But you brought it up."

That's when I looked at her clothes and her hands. "You did wash up before lunch, didn't you?"

She smirked at me. "Don't worry. They make us wear latex gloves and these hideous jumpsuits over our clothes. But thanks for asking."

"So how long will you be on potty detail?"

"Until the end of the month." She groaned. "If I don't kill myself first."

"I'm sorry."

"You and me both."

"But does it make you want to rethink your life?"

She shook her head stubbornly and popped a fry into her mouth. "Nope."

"Not even a little?"

"The only thing it makes me want is to have fun when the working's done." She grinned. "Not bad, huh?"

I let out an exasperated sigh.

"Oh, come on," she said. "You wouldn't deny a poor working girl the chance to cut loose and have some fun after a long week of scrubbing crud."

"There's nothing wrong with having fun," I told her. "Why don't you and I do something fun together?"

"Cool. Wanna come to the lake party with me tomorrow night?"

"That's not my idea of fun."

She feigned surprise. "Really?"

I just sipped my soda. Was there any way to reach this girl?

"Well, it's *my* idea of fun. And honestly, Maya, I don't see how you can judge me when you refuse to even give it a try."

"I could say the same of you. Why don't you give my kind of fun a try?"

"I have." She patted her mouth in a pretense of a yawn. "And it's boring. Besides, I think you just want me to hang with you so you don't feel bad about breaking up with Dominic."

And suddenly we were talking about that again. But there was no way I could make Marissa understand why I had done what I had done. And to be honest, by the time she finished with me, I was almost beginning to question it myself. Fortunately I am scheduled to meet with Caitlin tomorrow.

## August 16

"I heard you and Dominic had quite a fight last weekend." We'd barely sat down with our coffees before Caitlin cut right to the chase.

"How'd you hear that?"

She shrugged. "It's youth group, Maya. What do you think?"

I nodded. "Yeah, I should've known. Just the same, I'm not sorry." Then I filled her in on some of the details just in case the eavesdroppers didn't get it right.

"How did Dominic take it?"

"He actually accused me of thinking I was too good for him."

She kind of smiled. "That sounds familiar."

"Familiar?"

"It's a guy's way of protecting himself. Blame it on the girl. Josh did the same thing with me back in high school. Before he came around."

"But how did he come around? I mean, I realize he went to Bible college, but what about before that?"

"It took a while. But here's an idea."

"What?"

"I'll ask Josh to have a chat with him."

"But I don't want it to—"

"Josh won't mention our conversation, Maya. But since

Dominic is helping with worship and he and Josh get along, maybe Josh needs to spend more time with him."

"Kind of like you do with me?"

She nodded. "It's just one more way that Christians learn and grow. Jesus called it discipleship."

"Okay, I have one more question," I said hesitantly.

"Go for it."

"Well, I know I hurt Dominic."

"And?"

"I should probably ask him to forgive me."

She nodded.

"That's it?" I waited. "No advice on how to do that?"

"Just the same old, same old."

"Pray about it?"

"Yep." She grinned. "And you might want to read those verses I gave you again."

"While we're on the topic of those verses, Brooke's family is probably home from vacation now."

Caitlin waited.

"And I think God is telling me that, besides forgiving Brooke, I should tell her I'm sorry."

Caitlin's whole face lit up. "That's fantastic, Maya."

I frowned. "Why is that? I mean, the truth is, I'm dreading it. I don't even want to do it, but I think I need to. But why is it fantastic?"

"Because it's Christlike."

"Huh?"

"Jesus went to the cross for us, Maya."

"Meaning?"

"Meaning He didn't have to do it. He wasn't guilty of anything. But He took our sins on Himself, and by dying He secured
our forgiveness."

"Okay, I sort of know that. Or I'm learning about it. But I
don't see how that applies to Brooke and me."

"Because like you said, Brooke was the one who did the most
wrong. She lied and made you miserable. And my guess is that
she's miserable now. But you feel a tiny bit of responsibility, right?"

I nodded.

"For you to go to her... Well, I just know God is going to bless
you, Maya."

"Okay, now I have another question."

"What?"

"Will I ever reach that place where I'm not having to forgive
people or not having to ask them to forgive me?"

She laughed. "I hope not."

"Why?"

"Well, unless it's in heaven. I think that life on earth is always
going to be about forgiving and loving—it's just the way humans
are."

"Oh..." I nodded, trying to soak this in.

So on my way home, I pulled over and dialed Dominic's
number. I had to take care of this before youth group. No more

parking lot scenes for this girl. The phone rang a few times, and I wondered if he was avoiding me. Finally it went to his messaging, and I decided to just go for it.

"Hey, Dominic. I just wanted to tell you that I'm sorry for the way I handled everything last Saturday. But I can't pretend like everything is okay either. I really do like you. And I don't think I'm too good for you. But there are things about our relationship that make me uncomfortable. And if you can't accept that, I don't really see how we can be a couple. Anyway, I'm sorry if I hurt you. I think you're a cool guy. And I hope that someday we can talk. But no yelling, okay?" Then I said "bye" and hung up. Part of me thought this could be the chicken way out, but another part of me felt good. I had said what I felt and not gotten distracted. I wasn't angry. I was simply honest. And the ball was in his court now.

But Dominic wasn't at youth group tonight. Was it because of me? That thought made me sad. Later I wondered if Dominic, Brooke, and Amanda had all skipped youth group tonight because of me. Brooke and Amanda haven't been there for over a month. Then again, I may be taking myself too seriously. Or as Marissa would say, "Get over yourself, Maya." Of course, this only reminds me that she decided to go to that stupid lake party tonight. When will she learn?

## August 17

Kim woke me up early this morning. Odd, since it's Sunday, but I could tell by her creased brow that something was wrong.

"What's up?" I asked groggily.

"Dad just heard about it."

"What?" I sat up and waited.

"Marissa."

*"What?"*

"She's been in a really bad car wreck, Maya."

"How bad?" I whispered.

She didn't say anything, but tears filled her eyes, and her hands were shaking.

"How bad?" I asked again.

"Dad said that she's alive…but it doesn't look good."

Kim gave some more details about the accident, but her words just seemed to float over my head, and everything seemed blurry and unreal. And I just sat there in shock and sobbed, deep aching sobs.

I could hear Kim praying, but I wasn't sure I was even able. And then I stood up and yanked on my jeans and a sweatshirt and flip-flops. "Let's go!" I shouted at Kim.

"Where?"

"I've got to see Marissa." I wiped my wet face with my sleeve.

"I'll drive," she offered, and I didn't argue. As she drove to the hospital, we took turns praying for Marissa. And that's when I realized my cousin loves Marissa almost as much as I do. Even so, I know that Marissa has been closer to me than to Kim. And I hoped I'd be able to see her. I wasn't sure how bad she was, but I just wanted to talk to her. I just wanted to tell her that I loved her, that God loved her, and that it wasn't too late.

The receptionist told us that Marissa was still in ICU but that we could go to the waiting room up there. Marissa's dad, still in his cop uniform, was pacing back and forth and rubbing his hands together. A couple of other officers were sitting nearby with somber faces. Kim and I sat down across from them, and Kim asked if there was any news on Marissa.

"They're trying to stabilize her," one of the guys said with a hopeless look in his eyes.

"How long has she been here?" I asked.

"Since around two this morning," the other cop said.

"Was she driving?" I asked.

"No." Marissa's dad walked over to join us. "Her friend Eddie Valdez was driving. Driving Marissa's car."

"I'm so sorry," I said.

He just nodded and turned away.

"How is Eddie?" I asked the cops across from us.

"Better than Marissa. He had on his seat belt."

"Marissa was thrown from the car."

"Oh…" I glanced at Kim, and she reached over and took my hand.

"Among other things, she suffered a serious head injury." The policeman sighed and shook his head. "Pretty severe."

That's when the policemen introduced themselves as Officers Burns and Crandall. And Kim introduced us.

"How did you girls hear about it?" asked Burns. Kim explained that her dad was the editor of the newspaper.

"Oh, right, Allen Peterson," said Crandall. "Nice guy."

"Do you think there's any chance that we can see Marissa?" I asked, knowing it was probably useless. "Just for a minute?"

"They won't even let her dad in there yet."

"Do you think she'll…" My voice drifted off.

"Maya is Marissa's best friend," Kim explained. And although I wouldn't have laid claim to that title, I supposed it might be true. Marissa didn't have any other close friends. Not girls anyway.

"Hey, you're that green girl on TV, aren't you?" Burns said.

I nodded, but fresh tears were slipping out now.

"Well, Marissa is lucky to have such a good friend," Crandall said. Then he frowned. "Why weren't you with her tonight?" It wasn't an accusation. More just curious. Still, it made me mad.

"I wish I *had* been with her," I told him. "Then maybe this wouldn't have happened."

"Marissa's dad had warned her again and again about that—"

"That's right," said Adam, Marissa's dad. "But that's water under the bridge now."

"I know," said Crandall quickly. "I'm just saying you did all you could—"

"Did I?" Marissa's dad clenched his fists and shook them. "Did I really?" And then he broke down, collapsing onto a chair as his two buddies gathered around him, trying to show support. But really, what could they say? What could anyone say?

"Let's pray," Kim said quietly to me. And right there, just a few feet away from where Marissa's dad was sobbing, Kim began to pray out loud for Marissa. And her prayers were strong and full of faith. I joined her, hoping to have as much faith as she did. And before long, the policemen were praying too.

We stayed at the hospital all day, but Marissa's condition remained the same. Word spread quickly, and by noon a lot of people from our church had come, including Josh and Caitlin and Chloe. Not long after that, Allie and Laura and several more of their friends—kids who had known Marissa for years—showed up as well. About twenty or more of us were all crowded in the waiting room. And we were all praying. Amid this crowd was Dominic, and I could tell he'd been crying as well. Then I remembered that Eddie was his friend too.

Although my heart went out to Dominic, I wasn't ready to have a conversation with him yet. All I wanted to do was pray for Marissa. It's all I felt capable of doing. Nothing else mattered. Even now, as I sit in my room—emotionally drained and totally exhausted—writing in my journal because I can't sleep, I feel so helpless. All the things I've been worrying about seem minor now. All I can think about is Marissa and if she will live. The prognosis is not good. The doctor said she may not even make it through the night. Even so, I will keep praying. And I'll return to the hospital first thing in the morning, hoping for a miracle.

## August 18

I guess the miracle is that Marissa is still alive. No one expected her to make it through the night. Of course she's still unconscious, and she's got tubes and wires and all sorts of things keeping her stabilized. But she's still here—just barely.

This morning Marissa's dad was allowed five-minute "visits" with her. And by midafternoon, he asked if I wanted to see her too.

"Are you sure it's okay?" I'd heard it was "family only." Not that Marissa has much family.

He nodded. "Marissa really likes you, Maya."

"I want to talk to her."

He nodded again, sadly. "I'm not sure she can hear you, but it's worth a try. I've said a lot of things myself."

So, feeling unsure but determined, I went into the ICU area and let myself into her room. Swallowing back the shock of seeing her like this, so broken and helpless, I went to the side of her bed and simply began to talk.

"Marissa," I said slowly, "I'm so sorry this happened to you. But I need to tell you some things, okay? First of all, I need to say that I really, really love you. And I don't think I've actually said that before. But it's true. I love you. In some ways you've felt almost like a sister to me. Okay, a dysfunctional sister, but, hey, that's kind of like my family. But besides that, I want you to know that God loves you, Marissa. He really, really loves you. Even more than I do. And He sent His Son Jesus so that if you believe in Him, you will live forever."

Tears were coming down my cheeks now. "I don't want you to die, but I know it's a possibility. And if you're leaving the planet, I want to make sure you know where you're going. I want to make sure you accept God's love and His forgiveness. It's like I've told you before, Marissa, I couldn't live without it. And you can't die without it."

Now, it could've been my imagination, but I thought her eyelashes fluttered just then. It might've just been an involuntary twitch. Whatever it was, I didn't get to stay and find out because the nurse was motioning to me that my time was up.

"I love you, Marissa." I eased away from her bed. "But God loves you even more. I hope you're listening." By the time I closed the door behind me, I was crying hard. All I could do was return to the waiting room, where Kim and Chloe came over and hugged me.

"How do you think she's doing?" Chloe asked.

I shook my head. "I don't know."

I still don't know. By the time I left the hospital tonight, I knew only three things. Marissa is still alive. But she may not be alive tomorrow. All we can do is pray.

## Maya's Green Tip for the Day

My only green tip today is that I hope God can recycle Marissa back into a healthy girl. I hate to say it, but the way she lived has been wasteful—I'm afraid she may have wasted the most precious and unrenewable resource on the planet...herself.

# Nineteen

## August 23

This has been the longest week of my life. Kim and Uncle Allen encouraged me to get back to normal activities. At the time I couldn't even remember what normal was. But they were worried that I was getting depressed. Well, who wouldn't be depressed? Each day at the hospital was just like the day before. Nothing changed. Nothing improved. Although I prayed and prayed, there seemed no reason to hope.

Still, I think they were right. It has helped me to go back to work. I've visited Marissa in the mornings and then gone to Jacqueline's afterward. I even managed to do my news spots but only because the producer allowed me to mention my friend and ask for the community's prayers. I suppose I do need these distractions. I honestly don't know how Marissa's dad can bear it. He has been at the hospital 24/7, and in the past few days he has hardly left her side. When I confessed to him that I was having a tough time with all this, he wasn't a bit surprised. Then I told him that without God I wouldn't be able to endure it at all.

"Marissa told me you were a Christian," he said quietly. We were standing outside her room, waiting for the nurse to take her vitals and change her IV.

"Really?"

"Yes. Then she got mad at me when I suggested she should go to church with you." He shook his head. "I was always trying to change her."

"Or protect her."

He held up his hands. "Not that it helped."

"I am certain that Marissa loves you."

He seemed surprised. "I don't know why you'd say that. Marissa and I were always fighting over something. I'm sure she told you about it."

"She did. She also told me things that made me realize how much she cared about you."

I knew by his expression that he didn't believe me.

"That's the main reason she didn't want to go away to college."

He just stared at me now, shaking his head. "She said that?"

"Yes, it was a very private confession. But now that...well, I don't think she'd mind if I told you. She said that she knew you loved her but that you were trying too hard to make her toe the line."

"Probably why she rebelled so much."

"I don't know..."

"I do."

"If it's any consolation, I said some of the same kinds of things to her. She always accused me of lecturing her."

"But she considered you a friend."

"I considered her a friend too. I love Marissa." I was starting to cry again.

"I'm glad you were her friend, Maya." He had tears as well.

"But she's still here." I wanted to be hopeful. "She might make it."

"She *might*..." But I could tell as he said this, he didn't believe it. He'd given up.

"Thousands of people are praying for her, Mr. Phillips."

He nodded and then blew his nose. "Yes. I appreciate that."

I wanted to say something else, something more encouraging. But he just turned and slowly walked away. He looked defeated, like he'd been beaten.

The nurse finished, and with tears in my eyes, I went in to visit Marissa. But I didn't want her to know how discouraged I felt or how miserable her dad was just now. Not that she would really know. But just in case I kept my voice cheerful. And, as usual, I started out by talking naturally, like we were sitting at the mall having lunch together. Then I got more serious and told her how I loved her and how God loved her even more. And I read from the Bible—verses about believing in Jesus and eternal life. I told her about a place beyond death. A place that Jesus was preparing for us.

"But I really want you to stick around, Marissa. I need you. I want you to fight this and to get well. I am praying for a miracle. And lots of others are praying too. We want you back."

I continued talking, like I always do, just rambling on and on. Sometimes, like today, I feel silly, like I am fooling myself. Some of her other close friends, like Chloe and Allie, have been allowed to visit her too. And they've been doing the same thing. Although there's no way to know if she can hear any of this, we think it could help. And an older nurse named Carmen assured me that it could make a difference.

"I've talked to patients who recover from comas, and I'm amazed at how much they could perceive while they were unconscious," she told me a day or two ago. "The brain is a very mysterious thing."

"Do you think she'll wake up?" I asked hopefully.

"Only God knows, dear."

And I know that's true, but I'll admit that I'm getting impatient. At the same time, I'm glad Marissa is still here. I imagine her listening to us, trapped inside her motionless body, taking in our words and processing the Bible verses and our invitations to eternal life…and I try to believe that God is at work. I try to have faith. But it's not easy.

Sometimes I feel like I'm on an emotional roller-coaster ride of my own. I go through bouts of feeling guilty, like why didn't I say more to her? Why didn't I keep her from going to the lake party? Or why didn't I go with her and make sure she got safely home? Then I get angry and think, how is it fair that her selfish choices are now hurting everyone? Why does one person get to hold dozens of others hostage like this? Of course that just makes me feel guilty. How can I think such horrid thoughts when someone I love is so close to death? Then I get sad and wonder what it would feel like to be Marissa right now. Stuck in some kind of life-or-death limbo. And so I pray and try to muster up enough faith to move a mountain. Up and down and all around, I wonder when the ride will end.

But there have been a couple of bright spots in my week. On Wednesday morning at the hospital, Dominic took me aside to talk. Fortunately, he kept it short and sweet. I'm sure that's all I could take.

"I'm so sorry, Maya. I realize what a complete jerk I've been. And I'm really sorry. I hope you'll forgive me."

"I do forgive you," I said quickly. "And I'm sorry too."

"Yeah, I got your message. Thanks."

"And maybe…when things settle down…maybe we can talk about it."

He sighed. "Yeah, when things settle down. And just so you know, I'm going to be meeting with Josh on a weekly basis now. Kind of like you do with Caitlin."

I looked at him like this was a surprise. "That's cool."

"Yeah. I think I need to grow up some."

"I think we all do." I glanced over to the ICU area. "Marissa is a good reminder of that."

"Eddie's doing a lot better," he said.

"Yeah, I talked to him yesterday. Sounds like he'll be released in a few days."

"He's miserable over what happened to Marissa."

"I know. He told me that they'd both had too much to drink. But he convinced her that he was sober enough to drive." Just saying this made my eyes fill with tears. "I told Marissa so many times"—I choked on my words—"to be careful…not to go…that it was dangerous."

Dominic put his arms around me. Not in that passionate way, but in a pure brotherly hug, and I rested there awhile. Just crying.

"I'm sure Marissa wishes she'd listened," he said quietly.

"I just hope she's listening now."

The second bright spot in my week was when I ran into Brooke at the hospital. She was actually bringing a bouquet of flowers, but I could tell she was not happy to see me. It looked like she'd planned to just drop them off and go, but I decided to jump right in.

"Do you have a minute?" I asked.

"My mom's out in the car."

"Well, I can walk out to the car with you."

"That's okay," she said quickly. "I have a minute."

So we sat in the main lobby, and I began. "Look, I know this thing with the lawsuit turned into a real mess. And I'm pretty sure you regret faking a serious injury. But I wasn't exactly perfect either. I said some pretty mean things, and I don't think that's how Jesus would act. So I just want to say I'm sorry, Brooke. And I hope we can put it behind us."

She sat there staring at me with the blankest expression, and I was thinking she was about to say something really shallow and irritating. But instead she burst into tears.

"I'm so sorry," she sobbed. "I'm sorry I pretended to be injured. And I'm sorry that Marissa has been hurt like this. And I know I'm not a good Christian. And I'm just really, really sorry. Please forgive me."

To my surprise I actually hugged her. "I forgive you."

Then we both stood, and she wiped her wet face with her hands. "I'm praying for Marissa. Although I'm sure she would question that since she must've thought I was a terrible person. But I really am praying."

"I'll tell her that."

"Is she conscious?"

"No. But I talk to her all the time. I'm hoping she can hear."

Brooke nodded. "I hope so too."

So in a way some good has come out of this sadness. But I just really, really want Marissa to be okay. And even as I write this, I'm afraid I don't have enough faith. Every time I see her, she looks exactly the same—like she's never going to get better. But then I think, why is she still here? Is God keeping her here for a reason? Mostly I try not to think about it too much. It's better to just pray.

## August 31

It's been two weeks since Marissa and Eddie were in the wreck. Eddie is recovering at home and, according to Dominic, feeling pretty depressed and guilty. Marissa still hasn't regained consciousness, but the doctors are sounding a little more positive. They seem surprised that she's still here. Also, some of her injuries are healing. And Marissa's dad consulted with a neurosurgeon, and Marissa is now scheduled for surgery. So I'm feeling a smidgen of hope.

But today was a different kind of sad. Today I had to say good-bye to Kim. Because of the situation with Marissa, she's put it off, but now there's no time to spare, and she has to head off to college. I spent all morning helping her pack—actually cram—her stuff into the back of Uncle Allen's car. He's taking some days off from the paper so he can drive her to school.

"Are you sure you'll be okay on your own?" Kim asked me for about the tenth time as we were saying our final good-byes in the driveway.

I know she meant the situation with Marissa, because she and her dad have been worried that I'm taking it too hard, that I'm depressed. I don't think it's possible not to be sad, but I also think I'm dealing with it. I'm trying to trust God with the whole thing. So I put on a brave face and reminded Kim to pray about Marissa's neurosurgery next week.

"Really, I'm okay," I assured her one last time. "I'll be perfectly fine."

"Tell Marissa I'm praying for her," Kim said as she hugged me. "And for you too, Maya. Be strong."

"And we'll stay in touch," I promised. "I'll e-mail you every day."

"Same here." Then she hugged me again. "You're like a sister to me. I can't even say how thankful I am that you're in our lives." She stepped back and looked at me with teary eyes. "Look at me. Here I am telling you to be strong!"

"Have a good trip." I waved and smiled as they pulled out. But as soon as the car was out of sight, I felt like crying. Still, I reminded myself that I need to be even more mature now. For my uncle's sake as much as for my own.

Last week Uncle Allen pretty much reiterated what he'd said to my dad, that I was more than welcome to remain in their home. And he said it was an offer he didn't make lightly and that he appreciated that I was mature for my age.

"I'm not concerned that you'll pull any crazy adolescent stunts," he told me. "Not that I want you to feel pressured to be perfect. I know teens need to have some fun." He smiled. "But your sensibilities remind me so much of Kim that I'm not worried." He also said he considered me a part of the family, and that's something *I* don't take lightly.

But for however long I remain here, I so don't want to be a burden to my uncle. I want to stand on my own two feet. I want to do things right. All the upheaval of the past two weeks has helped me make some decisions. Most important, I have decided to do my senior year at Harrison High. I know I don't have to do this. I have my GED. But I just think it's what I need right now.

Kim and Uncle Allen were both hugely relieved when I told them. They agreed that it was the right choice. My dad felt the same. I will still work on getting my emancipation—not to have a place of my own but simply to keep Shannon from trying to get me back if she wins her appeal and is released from prison. And it's scheduled for the end of September, so I need to get busy.

## September 3

School started today. To my surprise, Brooke and Amanda asked to sit with me at lunch. Then Dominic joined us, along with Eddie, who is hobbling around on crutches and never smiles. I suppose we were a rather somber crowd. And I wondered what Marissa would think if she could see us. She was always such a cutup during lunch, so sarcastic and witty. She would put the spark into any conversation. Okay, sometimes it was a dark spark, but she would get people going.

"What's the latest on Marissa?" asked Amanda.

"She's been in neurosurgery this morning," I said. "They're supposed to finish by one."

"Everyone needs to pray for a real miracle," Brooke said as she stuck a straw in her soda.

"Why don't we pray for Marissa right now?" Dominic suggested.

"Right here?" Amanda looked over her shoulder to where kids were pushing and joking in the lunch line.

"Yeah," Eddie said in a gruff but loud voice. "Right here!"

Well, that surprised me, because I didn't think Eddie was even a Christian, but who knew? So we all bowed our heads and prayed. I overheard some jabs from kids passing by, teasing us for our public display of faith. But I don't think anyone at our table cared. We just kept praying—praying with enthusiasm, going around the table several times before we finished with a hearty "amen." Then I opened my eyes to see a girl I barely remembered from last year. She made a snooty face and said, "What is this, the church kids club? Are you going to sing a hymn now?"

Without smiling, I looked directly into her eyes. "We were praying for a friend of ours, Marissa Phillips; you might remember her. She graduated last year. But she was nearly killed in a wreck and is having brain surgery today." I paused for effect. "Maybe you'll want to pray for her too."

The girl seemed slightly shocked, but she just nodded and quickly moved away. Then Dominic gave me a little thumbs-up, and Eddie smiled ever so slightly.

I went straight to the hospital after school, but when I went to Marissa's room in ICU, the bed was empty. Her surgery had to be done by now, and suddenly I felt very afraid. What if something went wrong? What if Marissa was—

"Are you looking for Marissa?" It was Carmen, the older nurse who's been so encouraging.

"Yes. Where is she? Is she okay?"

The nurse smiled. "The surgery went well. She was in recovery for several hours, but her condition was stable enough that she's been moved to the regular inpatient unit."

"Is she conscious?" I asked hopefully.

Carmen shook her head. "No, not yet. But the surgery went well, so maybe…in time…" She told me Marissa's room number, and I went to the third floor and found her room. Mr. Phillips was just coming out.

"Oh, Maya." He seemed relieved to see me.

"How is she?"

He sighed. "She seems the same…but they say the surgery went as well as possible."

"Maybe it takes time."

He nodded. "Do you want to visit her while I get something to eat?"

"Sure."

"Her mother went back home about an hour after the surgery."

"Oh…" I knew he hadn't been that pleased when Marissa's mother had shown up, and he was probably glad that she was gone now. I had one brief conversation with her, and I could tell she felt guilty. I didn't think she'd be here long.

"I'll be back in about an hour," Mr. Phillips told me.

So I went into Marissa's new room. It was a relief to see her in a less intensive-looking place. Oh, she still had tubes and machines, and her head was bandaged, but she looked slightly more peaceful. That seems like a weird way to describe her, but she did look peaceful.

As usual, I just began talking to her. I told her about the first day of school, how we'd prayed for her and kids had made fun of us. "Kind of like you would've done," I said. "You've taken your share of potshots at Christians." I kind of laughed. "Not that I blame you. I've felt the same way. But just because Christians aren't perfect doesn't mean that God's not perfect. And He probably gets frustrated at the way we act sometimes. Or maybe, because He's God, He doesn't get frustrated." So I rambled on and on. Then when I knew my hour was coming to an end, I took her hand.

"Marissa, I really do love you." This is how I usually end our time. "And sometimes I feel guilty that I haven't been a better friend to you, but as you know, I'm not perfect either. I really do believe your life is in God's hands now because everyone is praying for you and because God loves you. And so I'm not going to worry about you—I'm just going to keep praying."

As I said this, I felt what seemed like the tiniest twitch of her fingers. "Did you just squeeze my hand? Can you hear me, Marissa?" I waited, and the tiny squeeze happened again. It was not a coincidence!

Just then her dad came back, and I told him what had happened. And it was so cool to see his eyes light up. "You think she can hear you?"

"I think so."

Now he came over and took her hand. "Marissa, sweetheart, can you hear me? I want you to know how much I love you. I want you to know that I will never try to force you to be something you aren't. I will accept you for who you are. Can you hear me?"

Then he looked over at me with a huge smile. "She squeezed my hand!"

And although that's all we got from her this afternoon—a gentle squeeze of the hand—I believe it's the beginning. I believe she's coming back. And I believe that God is doing a miracle.

Now I've come to the last page of this diary, and although it's hard to end this volume while my friend still hangs in the balance, I feel certain that, one way or another, Marissa is going to be okay. I can't even explain why I feel so sure, whether it's because of the hand squeeze or simply because I know God is at work. But I do believe God is up to something—something big. I expect something miraculous is going to happen with Marissa, and I know something miraculous is happening in me. And I feel very hopeful for the school year ahead of me. Oh, I know there will be more bumps in the road, but with God at the wheel, it'll be a great ride.

## Maya's Green Tip for the Day

Don't forget that God is the Great Recycler. He can recycle your heartache into strength. He can recycle a hurt relationship into a healthy one. He can recycle your lostness into being found. He can recycle your strife into peace. And He is ready to recycle whatever you want to give Him. So what are you waiting for?

Readers Group
Guide

1. After becoming a Christian, Maya wants to change. What motivates you to make changes in your life?

2. Why do you think Maya is more comfortable with Marissa than some of her Christian "friends"?

3. As a believer, Maya is as committed as ever to being green. How do you feel about conservation? What steps do you take to help care for the planet?

4. Why is it so important for Maya to meet regularly with Caitlin? Have you ever been involved in a mentoring relationship? Explain.

5. Maya doesn't like that Marissa parties and drinks, yet she continues to be friends with her. Do you think that's okay? Why or why not?

6. Do you think Maya was right to break up with Dominic? Why or why not?

7. Maya doesn't really want to have any contact with her mom, Shannon. If you were Maya's friend, how would you advise her?

8. Brooke is a piece of work and a huge challenge for Maya. Do you have anyone like Brooke in your life? If so, how do you deal with him or her?

9. Maya is still undecided about seeking emancipation from her parents. What would you do if you were in her shoes?

10. Were you surprised when Marissa was seriously injured in the car wreck? What do you think is going to happen to her now? Why?